THE WORKS OF LIANG YUCHUN

梁遇春

著译全集

2

第二卷

李力夫 商昌宝 主编

海峡出版发行集团 | 福建教育出版社

本卷总目

A Gem of English Essays
英国小品文选 ………………………………………… 1

A Gem of English Essays
英国小品文选

（英汉对照）

梁遇春　译注

"开明英汉译注丛书"之一，开明书店，1932年5月初版

CONTENTS

目　次

译者序 ·· 5

Richard Steele（1672—1729）

Mr. Bickerstaff Visits a Friend

毕克司达夫先生访友记 ································· 8

Joseph Addison（1672—1719）

On the Excessive Care of Health—Letter of the Valetudinarian

论健康之过虑——虚弱者之来信 ············· 28

Oliver Goldsmith（1728—1774）

The Man in Black

黑衣人 ·· 42

Charles Lamb（1775—1834）

Detached Thoughts on Books and Reading

读书杂感 ·· 56

William Hazlitt（1778—1830）

On the Feeling of Immortality in Youth

青年之不朽感 ·· 86

Leigh Hunt（1784—1859）

Watchmen

更夫 ·· 116

Logan Pearsall Smith（1865— ）

The Rose

玫瑰树 ·· 142

W. H. Hudson（1841—1922）

The Samphire Gatherer

采集海草之人 ··· 152

Robert Lynd（1879— ）

This Body

躯体 ·· 168

Sir Walter Raleigh（1861—1922）

Don Quixote

吉诃德先生 ··· 188

译者序

  把Essay这字译做"小品",自然不甚妥当。但是Essay这字含义非常复杂,在中国文学里,带有Essay色彩的东西又很少,要找个确当的字眼来翻,真不容易。只好暂译做"小品",拿来和Bacon,Johnson,以及Edmund Gosse所下Essay的定义比较一下,还大致不差。希望国内爱读Essay的人,能够想出个更合式的译法。

  在大学时候,除诗歌外,我最喜欢念的是Essay。对于小说,我看时自然也感到兴趣,可是翻过最后一页以后,我照例把它好好地放在书架后面那一排,预备以后每星期用拂尘把书顶的灰尘扫一下,不敢再劳动它在我手里翻身打滚了。Hawthorne的《红字》(*The Scarlet Letter*),Dostoevski的《罪与罚》(*Crime and Punishment*),Conrad的 *Lord Jim*, *The Nigger of Narcissus* 都是我最爱念的小说,可是现在都安然地躺在家里我父亲的书架上面了。但是 Poe，Tennyson，Christina Rossetti，Keats 的诗集；Montaigne，Lamb，Goldsmith 的全集；Steele，Addison，Hazlitt，Leigh Hunt，Dr. Brown，De Quincey，Smith，Thackeray，Stevenson，Lowell，Gissing，Belloc，Lewis，Lynd 这些作家的小品集却总在我的身边，轮流地占我枕头旁边的地方。心里烦闷的时候，顺手拿来看看，总可医好一些。其中有的是由旧书摊上买来而曾经他人眉批目注过的，也有是贪一时便宜，板子坏到不能再坏的；自然，也有十几本金边大字印度纸印的。我却一视同仁，读惯了也不想再去换本好板子的来念，因为恐怕有忘恩背义的嫌疑。

常常当读得入神时候，发些痴愿。曾经想把 Montaigne 那一千多页的小品全翻作中文，一回浊酒三杯后，和一位朋友说要翻 Lamb 全集，并且逐句加解释，第二天澄心一想，若使做出来，岂不是有些像《皇清经解》，把顽皮万分的 Lamb 这样拘束起来，Lamb 的鬼晚上也会来口吃地和我吵架了。有时高兴起来，也译一二篇，但将译文同原文一比较，免不了觉得失望。所以天天读，天天想翻，二三年始终没有办到。前年冬天反麻麻糊糊地译出一篇自己不十分爱读的屠格涅夫（Turgenev）的小说。回想起来，笑也不是，叹气也不是，只好不去想罢！

今年四五月的时候，心境沉闷，想作些翻译解愁。到苦雨斋和岂明老人商量，他说若使用英汉对照地出版，读者会更感到有趣味些。我觉这法子很好，就每天伏案句斟字酌地把平时喜欢的译出来。先译十篇，做个试验，译好承他看一遍，这些事我都要感谢他老先生。

本来打算每一个作家，都加一篇评传，但是试写Lamb评传，下笔不能自已，写了一万字，这样算起六篇评传就占六万字了，（当代小品文四篇，本不拟作评传，只打算做一篇，泛论当代的小品文，）比翻译还要多二万字，道理说不过去，所以也就不做，等将来再说罢。

所加注释，除原文困难的地方以外，许多是顺便讨论小品文的性质同别的零零碎碎的话，所以有不少赘言，不过也免得太干燥，英文程度好，用不着注释的人，也可以拿来看看。

译这书时，我是在北京马神庙西斋；现在写这些话时，人却在真茹了。而且北京也改作北平了。

译得不妥的地方，希望读者告诉我。

　　　　　　　　　　　　遇春　十七年九月五日

Richard Steele
(1672—1729)

Mr. Bickerstaff[1] Visits a Friend

There are several persons who have many pleasures and entertainments in their possession, which they do not enjoy. It is, therefore, a kind and good office to acquaint them with[2] their own happiness, and turn their attention to[3] such instances of their good fortune as

---

1 Mr. Bickerstaff: 这是 Steele 编 *Tatler* 时用的假名。这个名字倒有一段很有趣味的历史。在十八世纪开头那几年，伦敦有一位名气很大的星相专家，名叫 John Partridge；他每年出版一本历书，预言一年里的大事情。不幸得很，在他正交好运的时节，偏来了一位刁钻古怪，专爱捣乱的 Swift——做 *Gulliver's Travels* 和 *Tale of a Tub* 的 Swift——和他开玩笑。在1707年，Swift 用 Isaac Bickerstaff 这个假名，也印行一部历书，叫做 *Bickerstaff Almanac*（毕克司达夫历书），书里有照着天上星宿算出的关于1708年的预言。这章预言就是底下这几句刻毒嘲笑的话："我第一个预言是无关紧要的，但是我要说出来，证明那班自命为星相专家的人对自己事情都是不明白的，我的预言是关于做历书的 Partridge，我把他生时天上所照他的星宿

毕克司达夫先生访友记

有些人有许多快乐同玩意儿在他们的手头,他们自己却没有享受。所以有谁把他们本有的幸福说给他们听,使他们注意那容易忽略的好运气事情,这倒是一件仁爱的好事。结婚了的

拿来算了一下,算出他在三月二十九晚上十一时会发狂热病而死;所以我劝他留心些,把一切事情先期安排好罢!"三月三十那天,Swift 在报上登出 Partridge 死的消息,将他死的情形说得详详细细;过了一天,又有一篇堂皇典雅的哀诗。这么一来,谁也相信 Partridge 已经死了,自然没有人再去算命。Partridge 赶紧登报否认;Swift 也作篇文章来辩护自己,说根据星相的原理算来,Partridge 是死了,现在登报声明的这个人,是想冒名顶替的骗子,把 Partridge 弄得哑子吃黄连说不出苦来。Steele 的 *Tatler* 是在 1709 年发刊,正是 Isaac Bickerstaff 历书这件事传遍伦敦的时候,所以 Steele 把这个名字拿来做他的笔名。

2　acquaint with:inform 通知。
3　turn their attention to:direct their attention to 使他们注意。

they are apt to overlook. Persons in the married state often want such a monitor; and pine away their days, by looking upon the same condition in anguish and murmur, which[1] carries with it in the opinion of others a complication of all the pleasures of life, and a retreat from its inquietudes.

I am led into this thought by a visit I made an old friend, who was formerly my school-fellow.[2] He came to town last week with his family for the winter,[3] and yesterday morning sent me word his wife expected me to dinner[4]. I am, as it were[5], at home at that house, and every member of it knows me for their well-wisher. I cannot indeed express the pleasure it is, to be met by the children with so much joy as I am when I go thither. The boys and girls strive[6] who shall come first, when they think it is I that am knocking at the door; and that child which loses the race[7] to me runs back again to tell the father it is Mr. Bickerstaff. This day I was led in by a pretty girl, that[8] we all thought must have forgotten me; for the family has been

---

1 which: 此字之 antecedent 是前行的 the same condition。

2 I am led into this thought by a visit I made an old friend, who was formerly my school-fellow: 此句亦可译作"我去拜会一位老朋友——我从前的同学——因此我联想起这种意思"（就是前一个 paragraph 的意思）。这样译可以把"I am led into this thonght"这句原文弄得容易懂些，但是失之拘泥生硬。

3 He came... for the winter: 英国有钱人家多半夏天到海边或山上去避暑，冬天就到大都会去过冬，因为那时候城里特别热闹。

人们常需要这么一个教导者；他们看着自己的单调不变的生活情形，悲闷着喃喃埋怨，愁苦地度过他们的时光，但是由别人看来，他们的生活却包含着人生上一切快乐的综合，又是远离人生各种苦痛的躲难所。

我所以想到这点是由于去拜会一个老朋友，他是我的旧同学。前星期他同家眷到城里来过冬，昨天早上他打发人来，说他的妻子请我去列席宴会。我在他屋里同在自己家里一样随便，他们一家人都知道我心里是希望他们好的。我到的时候，孩子们是那么高兴地来迎接，我当时的快乐真是说不出来。当他们猜出打门者是我的时候，他们争先恐后跑出来；跑输了的小孩赶紧回转去告诉他的父亲，说毕克司达夫先生来了。这回是一个美丽的小姑娘带我进去，我们起初以为她一定不认识我了，

---

4 expected me to dinner：可以译作"等我去吃饭"。
5 as it were：仿佛是。
6 strive：contend with one another 竞争。
7 lose the race: fail in the race.
8 that：此字之 antecedent 是 a pretty girl。

out of town these two years. Her knowing me again was a mighty[1] subject with us, and took up[2] our discourse at the first entrance. After which, they began to rally me upon a thousand little stories[3] they heard in the country, about my marriage to one of my neighbour's daughters. Upon which the gentleman, my friend, said, "Nay, if Mr. Bickerstaff marries a child of any of his old companions, I hope mine shall have the preference; there is Mrs. Mary[4] is now sixteen, and would make him as fine a widow as the best of them[5]. But I know him too well; he is so enamoured with the very memory of those[6] who flourished in our youth, that he will not so much as look upon the modern beauties. I remember, old gentleman, how often you went home in a day to refresh your countenance and address when Teraminta[7] reigned in your heart. As we came up in the coach, I repeated to my wife some of your verses on her." With such reflec-

---

1 mighty: great.

2 took up: occupied.

3 a thousand little stories：不过说有许多的小故事，所谓"一千多个"自然是个"艺增"。

4 Mrs. Mary：在十八世纪 Anne 女皇时代，只有十岁以下的小女孩叫做 miss，大些的姑娘都叫做 mistress 或 madam。Richardson, Fielding 小说里面的称呼也都是这样。

5 and would make... of them：这句意思是说 Bickerstaff 年纪很大，嫁给他的人免不了会做孀妇。

因为他们一家不到城来已经有了两年。她居然还认得我，这变做我们谈天的一个大题目，我一进门就谈这件事情。这说完了，他们和我开玩笑，说出成千成万关于我同一个邻人的女孩结婚的小故事，这些都是他们在乡下听到的。那位先生，我的朋友，就说，"不对，若使毕克司达夫先生娶他朋友的女孩，我希望我的孩子会优先被选；这位玛利姑娘现在十六岁了，嫁给他将来定可做个再好不过的孺妇。但是我十分知道他，我晓得他的心给我们年青时节那班社会之花的影子迷住着呢。他对现在的美人连瞧一眼都不瞧。老朋友，我记得当宅拉敏达占住你的心时，你一天中多么常常回家去洗脸换衣服。当我们来城坐在车中，我还背诵出几首你赞她的诗，给我妻子听了"。这样子回想些久

---

6 those：指那时的美人（those beauties）。

7 Teraminta：这是个意大利的名字。十七八世纪的文人爱用意大利名字来叫他们所喜欢的女子，如 Swift 把常和他通信的二位女子 Miss Johnson 同 Miss Vanhomrigh 叫做 Stella 同 Vanessa。

tions on little passages[1] which happened long ago, we passed our time, during a cheerful and elegant meal. After dinner, his lady left the room, as did also the children. As soon as we were alone, he took me by the hand; "Well, my good friend," says he, "I am heartily glad to see thee; I was afraid you would never have seen all the company that dined with you to-day again. Do not you think the good woman of the house a little altered since you followed her from the play-house, to find out who she was, for me?" I perceived a tear fall down his cheek as he spoke, which moved me[2] not a little. But to turn the discourse, I said, "She is not indeed quite that creature she was, when she returned me the letter I carried from you; and told me, 'She hoped, as I was a gentleman, I would be employed no more to trouble her, who had never offended me; but would be so much the gentleman's friend, as to dissuade him from a pursuit, which he could never succeed in.' You may remember, I thought her in earnest[3]; and you were forced[4] to employ your cousin. Will[5], who made his sister get acquainted with her, for you. You cannot expect

---

1 passages: events that pass between persons or episodes 这个字作这样解时，常用复数。
2 moved me: touched my heart.
3 in earnest: seriously 真真出乎本心的。
4 you were forced: you were compelled 逼得你不得不。
5 Will: William 的简略叫法。英国人对于很熟的人，多半不说全名，

已过去的零碎事情，我们快乐地吃了精美的大餐。吃完了后，他的太太同小孩们全都离开房子。他们一走去，只有我们两个人在的时候，他就拉着我的手，说："我的好朋友，看见你，我心里非常愉快；我曾担忧过你也许不能再和我们全家像今天吃饭这样相会了。你觉得我们这好主妇同你从前由戏院出来跟着她走去，替我找出她的姓名的时候，有什么变更没有？"他说话时，我看见一滴眼泪由他的面颊流下，这很感动了我。因为要故意转过话路，我说："她同从前实在有些不同，那时她退还我代你送的信，口里说道：'因为我是上等社会人，她希望我不要再被人利用来和她捣乱，她并未曾得罪我过；请我好意劝那位朋友不要再干这万不会成功的事情。'你或者还记得，那时我以为她所说的是出于真心；你于是不得不找你表哥老威设法，他叫他的姊妹为了你同她结识。你不能希望她老是十五岁那么年

而用名字的一部分，如 Elizabeth 叫做 Bessy，Thomas 叫做 Tom，所以此处译做"老威"。

her to be for ever fifteen". "Fifteen!" replied my good friend: "Ah! you little understand, you that have lived a bachelor¹, how great, how exquisite a pleasure there is, in being really beloved! It is impossible, that the most beauteous face in nature should raise in me² such pleasing ideas, as when I look upon that excellent woman. That fading in her countenance³ is chiefly caused by her watching with me in my fever. This was followed by a fit of sickness, which had liked to have carried her off ⁴ last winter. I tell you sincerely, I have so many obligations to her, that I cannot, with any sort of moderation⁵, think of her present state of health. But as to what you say of fifteen, she gives me every day pleasures beyond what I ever knew in the possession of her beauty, when I was in the vigour of youth. Every moment of her life brings me fresh instances of her complacency⁶ to my inclinations, and her prudence in regard to my fortune.

---

1 you that have lived a bachelor: 凡是做小品文章的人，多数都装说自己是个单身汉，而且是饱经世故的老人，因为单身汉同老头子对于一切事情常有种特别的观察点，说起话来也饶风趣。以讽刺小说著名的Thackeray做他的小品 *Essaykin* 时候，自称是个老人（oldster），是个鳏夫，说出话也蔼然仁者之言，谁念他那本小品集 *Roundabout Papers*，总感到《虚荣市》和 *Henry Esmond* 的作者也有他温和慈祥的时候。说也奇怪，爱做小品的人，许多却真是单身汉，Goldsmith, Cowper, Lamb, Irving 等都是没有娶过亲的。

2 raise in me: give me.

3 that fading in her countenance: Bickerstaff的朋友是说他夫人病后体

青。""十五岁！"我朋友答道："啊！你这过独身生活的人简直不能了解真真被人家爱的快乐是多么广大而甜蜜呀！天地间最美丽的脸貌，不能像我看到这好妇人的时候似的，在我心中引起同样的快感。她脸上颜色的衰老多半是因为我生热病时她看护着劳苦了的缘故。跟着她也病倒了，这病去冬差一点就要把她带走。我老实告诉你，我感激她的地方太多，我对她现在的康健免不了万分关心。至于你所说的十五岁，她现在每天给我的快乐，是从前她美丽还在我也年富力强的时候，我所没有尝到的。现在她每时刻给我新例子，证明她是多么顺从我的癖好，对我家产是多么节俭留心。由我的眼睛看来，她的容貌比我头

弱，形容憔悴，恐怕活不得多久；但Bickerstaff看见他那种耽心愁苦的样子，故意装作听错话，回答说，一个人免不得会老，青春是不能常留的。fading: losing beauty and growing pale.

4 to have carried her off: to have been fatal to her 就是"她去冬害一场病，差一点病死"；因为中国人说人死，也有用"带走"，所以此处按字直译。

5 with any sort of moderation: with any kind of limitation.

6 complacency: the disposition to please or complaisance 殷勤。

Her face is to me much more beautiful than when I first saw it; there is no decay in any feature, which I cannot trace, from the very instant it was occasioned by some anxious concern for my welfare and interests. Thus, at the same time, methinks, the love I conceived towards her for what she was, is heightened by my gratitude for what she is. The love of a wife is as much above the idle passion commonly called by that name, as the loud laughter of buffoons is inferior to the elegant mirth of gentlemen. Oh, she is an inestimable jewel[1]. In her examination of her household affairs, she shows a certain fearfulness to find a fault[2], which makes her servants obey her like children, and the meanest[3] we have has an ingenuous[4] shame for an offence, not always to be seen in children in other families. I speak freely to you, my old friend; ever since her sickness, things that gave me the quickest[5] joy before, turn[6] now to a certain anxiety. As the children play in the next room, I know the poor things[7] by their steps, and am considering what they must do, should they lose their mother in their tender years[8]. The pleasure I used to take in telling my boy stories of battles, and asking my girl questions about the

---

1 Oh, she is an inestimable jewel: 意思是从前只看她的容貌美丽，现在却知道她对他情真意挚，所以比从前更爱她了。

2 to find a fault: to discover a fault 发现出错处。

3 the meanest: the meanest servant.

4 ingenuous: sincere 出乎本心的。

一次看她时还美；她脸上的衰老处，我都能由现出那时候起，说出这是那一回她对我的安宁上的大关心所引起的。所以同时我觉得从前对那过去的她的爱情是被我对现在的她的感谢增加热度了。妻子的爱和平常一般叫做爱的无聊情绪一比较，有雅人的秀美微笑与小丑的粗声狂笑的不同。啊！她是无价之宝。她管理家事，只怕找到别人的错处；这样子她使仆人像小孩一样地顺从她；我们最低级的仆人做错了事，都有自觉羞耻之心，那在别家小孩子里有时还找不出。我坦白地对你说，老朋友，从她那回病后，以前给我极端快乐的东西，现在倒使我烦恼。譬如小孩子在隔壁房子玩的时候，我由那脚步的声音，认出是这班可怜的小孩，心里就盘算，若他们在稚年失去了母亲，他们怎样办呢。以后我讲打仗故事给男孩听，问女孩洋囡囡的现

---

5 quickest: keenest.
6 turn: become.
7 poor things: the children.
8 tender years：身体未完全发达，尚需人照顾的时候。

disposal of her baby[1], and the gossiping of it, is turned into inward reflection[2] and melancholy."

He would have gone on[3] in this tender way, when the good lady entered, and with an inexpressible sweetness in her countenance told us, "she had been searching her closet for something[4] very good, to treat such an old friend as I was." Her husband's eyes sparkled with pleasure at the cheerfulness of her countenance; and I saw all his fear vanish in an instant. The lady observing something in our looks which showed we had been more serious than ordinary, and seeing her husband receive her with great concern under a forced cheerfulness[5], immediately guessed at what we had been talking of; and applying herself to me[6], said with a smile, "Mr. Bickerstaff, do not believe a word of what he tells you; I shall still live to have you for my second[7], as I have often promised you, unless he takes more care of himself than he has done since his coming to town. You must know, he tells me that he finds London is a much more healthy place than the country; for he sees several of his old acquaintance and school-fellows are here, young fellows with fair full-bottomed

---

1 her baby: her doll.
2 inward reflection: 肚里自己思念盘想。
3 would have gone on: would have continued to talk.
4 something: 一种神气。
5 a forced cheerfulness: an unnatural cheerfulness.

状,同它和她谈了什么话没有等各种快乐全变作心里的思虑同愁闷了。"

他正要这么悱恻地往下说,我们的好太太进来了,面上现着说不出的甜蜜告诉我们,"她刚在自己房里找些非常好的东西,来招待像我这样子的一个老朋友。"她丈夫看她笑容满面,喜欢得眼睛发光;我看见他的恐惧立刻烟消云散了。这位太太由我们脸上的神情觉察出刚才我们有特别严重的谈论,看了她丈夫的强为欢笑,很担心地同她招呼的样子,就立刻猜出我们谈的是什么东西;微笑地向我说:"毕克司达夫先生,他告诉你的话,一点也信不得,若使他对身体只管像到城以后这么不小心,我真是常常允许你似的,可以活到再嫁给你。你要知道,他对我说他觉得伦敦这地方比乡下更卫生得多;因为他看见有好几位老朋友旧同学在这里还是很年青,美丽的假发后面有着

---

6 applying herself to me: putting herself close to me.
7 second: second husband.

periwigs[1]. I could scarce keep him in this morning from going out open-breasted[2]." My friend, who is always extremely delighted with her agreeable humour, made her sit down with us. She did it with that easiness which is peculiar to women of sense[3]; and to keep up[4] the good humour she had brought in with her, turned her raillery upon me. "Mr. Bickerstaff, you remember, you followed me one night from the play-house; suppose you should carry me thither tomorrow night, and lead me into the front box." This put us into a long field of discourse about the beauties, who were mothers to the present[5], and shined in the boxes twenty years ago. I told her, "I was glad she had transferred so many of her charms[6], and I did not question but her eldest daugher was within half-a-year of being a toast."[7]

We were pleasing ourselves with this fantastical[8] preferment of the young lady, when on a sudden[9] we were alarmed with the noise of a drum, and immediately entered my little godson to give me a point of war[10]. His mother, between laughing and chiding, would

---

　　1 fair full-bottomed periwigs：十八世纪上等社会的人，都戴着假发（periwig），所谓 full-bottomed，就是在假发里面有满头的真发。
　　2 open-breasted：胸前没有扣紧，故意学年青人的样子。
　　3 women of sense：sensible women 通达事理的女人。
　　4 keep up：maintain 保持。
　　5 the present: the present beauties.
　　6 she had transferred so many of her charms：意思是她现在有这么多娇憨可爱的姑娘，而且个个都长得像她年青时节那样美丽。

满头的真发。今早我差不多不能阻止他打开着胸扣到街上去。"

我的朋友一向非常爱她这种有趣的滑稽，便叫她陪我们坐下。她态度雍容地坐下，这态度是聪明女人特别有的；为着要保持她带来的快乐空气，她转过来同我开玩笑。"毕克司达夫先生，你记得你有一夜从戏院里跟我一同出来的；你明晚带我往那里去，领我去前排坐，好不好。"这话引起了我们大谈一会现在已经做了母亲，而二十年前在戏厢里出过风头的美人。我同她说："我看着很高兴，她把她的许多美丽传了下来，我相信无疑，在半年之内她的大女孩子一定会变做被人举杯祝饮的姑娘了。"

我们正在把这位姑娘的幻想的高升拿来说笑，忽然间我们被鼓声吓住了，立刻走进我的教子，要给我奏一曲军歌。他的母亲半笑半骂地要把他赶出，可是我不肯就这样子同他分开了。

---

7 I did not question... of being a toast：英国习俗，年青人在酒酣耳热时，常高举酒杯，祝当时美人的健康，一饮而尽，在座的也陪饮。

8 fantastical：whimsical or fanciful 幻想的。

9 on a sudden: suddenly.

10 a point of war：a strain of martial music 一曲军歌。

have put him out of the room; but I would not part with him so. I found, upon conversation with him, thought he was a little noisy in his mirth, that the child had excellent parts[1], and was a great master of all the learning on the other side of eight years old[2]. I perceived him a very great historian in *Aesop's Fables*: but he frankly declared to me his mind, "that he did not delight in that learning, because he did not believe they were true"; for which reason I found he had very much turned his studies, for about a twelve-month past, into the lives and adventures of Don Belianis of Greece, Guy of Warwick, the Seven Champions[3], and other historians of that age. I could not but observe the satisfaction the father took in the forwardness of his son; and that these diversions might turn to some profit, I found the boy had made remarks, which might be service to him during the course of his whole life. He would tell you the mismanagements of John Hickerthrift, find fault with the passionate temper in Bevis of Southampton, and loved Saint George[4], for being the champion of England; and by this means had his thoughts insensibly moulded into the notions of discretion, virtue, and honour. I was extolling his accomplishments, when the mother told me, "that the little girl who

---

1 excellent parts: excellent ability 这样用时，part 常居复数。
2 on the other side of eight years old: less than eight years old 八岁以内。

同他谈起,我才知道他高兴时候,虽然有些吵闹,他有他的好本领,凡是八岁以内小孩所知道的学问他全懂得。我发现出他是《伊索寓言》的历史大家:但是他明白地告诉我他的意见,他不爱这门学问,因为他不相信那些事是真的;因此我晓得在最近一年他念的东西多半是"希腊的白里安力斯先生","瓦轶的葛勇士","七豪杰"同这么大年纪要看的别个历史家。我察出他父亲对儿子的大胆出众很满意;至于这种娱乐对他是有益的,我由他的批评里看出,那些话他一生都用得着。他会告诉你约翰·黑曲术利夫提处理事情不对的地方,对于撒生敦的毕比斯的坏脾气表示不满意,爱敬圣乔治,因为他是英国的保护神;这样子他的意思渐渐不知不觉地在谨慎,道德同名誉各个观念的模型里镕成。我赞美他的能干,他母亲对我说,今早邀

---

3 Don Belianis of Greece, Guy of Warwick, the Seven Champions 这些都是英国小孩常看的故事里英雄(nursery worthies)的名字。

4 Saint George:是英国的保护神(the patron saint of England)。

led me in this morning was in her way¹ a better scholar than he. Betty," said she, "deals chiefly in² fairies and sprights; and sometimes in a winter-night will terrify the maids with her accounts, until they are afraid to go up to bed."

I sat with them until it was very late, sometimes in merry, sometimes in serious discourse, with this particular pleasure, which gives the only true relish³ to all conversation, a sense⁴ that every one of us liked each other. I went home, considering the different conditions of a married life and that of a bachelor, and I must confess it struck me with secret concern⁵ to reflect that, whenever I go off⁶, I shall leave no traces behind me. In this pensive mood I returned to my family; that is to say, to my maid, my dog, and my cat⁷, who only can be the better or worse⁸ for what happens to me.

---

1 in her way: 在她所爱读的书那一方面。
2 deal in: 关心于。
3 relish: attractive quality 趣味。
4 sense: feeling.
5 concern: 耽心。
6 go off: die 死，即"离开此世界"之意。
7 to my maid, my dog, and my cat: 没有妻子儿女的意思。
8 the better or worse: 变好或者转坏。

我进来那小女孩在她自己方面比他还渊博。她说倍蒂多半注意神仙鬼怪的事；有时在冬夜把女仆都吓得不敢去睡觉。

我同他们坐到很迟才散，有时讲些快乐的话，有时正经地谈论，始终有一种特别的快乐，这快乐使一切谈天真正发生乐趣，就是我们大家都觉得有一种互相亲爱的情调。我回家，心里想着结婚生活和独身生活不同的地方；我不妨老实说，想起无论什么时候我一死去，没有一点痕迹留在后面，这情形使我暗暗地焦心。抱着这沉思的心境，我回到我的家庭；所谓家庭者就是我的女仆，我的狗儿同我的猫儿，我的境遇如何只对他们才有好坏的影响。

【附注】Steele 做这篇文章后过了半月，又写一篇"续篇"，*Mr. Bickerstaff Visits a Friend*（continued），叙述 Bickerstaff 朋友的太太死时的情形，但是写得太凄惨了，有故意使人掉眼泪的毛病，终不如这篇轻描淡写，漫话一日聚会的含蓄生姿。

Joseph Addison
(1672—1719)

On the Excessive Care of Health
—Letter of the Valetudinarian[1]

The following letter will explain itself[2] and needs no apology.

"Sir,

"I am one of that sickly tribe[3] who are commonly known by the name of Valetudinarians[4]; and do confess to you, that I first contracted[5] this ill habit of body, or rather of mind, by the study of physic. I no sooner began to peruse books of this nature, but I found my pulse was irregular; and scarce ever read the account of any disease that I did not fancy myself afflicted with. Dr. Sydenham's

---

1 这封信也是 Addison 自己写的,十八世纪写小品文字的作家常喜欢虚做一封来信,后面再加按语,用这法子可以将一件事情的正反两面都写出来,既没有用辩说体那样枯燥,比起对话体,文情又有从容不迫,娓娓清谈之致,不像那样针锋相对,没有闲逸的风味。Addison 同 Steele 最爱用这种布局。

2 will explain itself: 能够自己解释,就是一看便明白的意思。

论健康之过虑
——虚弱者之来信

下面的信一看就明白,用不着什么声明。

"先生:

"我是通常所谓身体虚弱这类多病人中间的一个;让我老实地告诉你,我是由读医学才得到这种身体的——倒可以说,心理的——坏习惯。我一开始读这类书,就觉得我的脉不对;差不多没有念过关于任何病的叙述,而自己不以为正患这个病。

---

3 tribe: class.

4 valetudinarian:这字含有身体没有什么大毛病,而自己心里却老以为有好多病的意思;同精神病人有些相同。写信的人也有点自知是神经过敏,常常有杯弓蛇影,自寻烦恼的地方,所以或者不过属于一种 ill habit of mind。

5 contracted:formed 得到。

learned treatise of fevers threw me into a lingering hectic, which hung upon me[1] all the while I was reading that excellent piece. I then applied myself[2] to the study of several authors, who have written upon phthisical distempers, and by that means fell into a consumption; till at length, growing very fat, I was in a manner[3] shamed out of that imagination. Not long after this I found in myself all the symptoms of the gout except pain[4]; but was cured of it by a treatise upon the gravel, written by a very ingenious author, who (as it is usual for physicians to convert one distemper into another) eased me of the gout by giving me the stone. I at length[5] studied myself into a complication of distempers; but accidentally taking into my hand that ingenious discourse written by Sanctorius, I was resolved to direct myself by a scheme of rules which I had collected from his observations. The learned world[6] are very well acquainted with that gentleman's invention; who, for the better carrying out of his experiments, contrived a certain, mathematical chair, which was so artificially hung upon springs, that it would weigh anything as well as a pair of scales. By this means he discovered how many ounces of his food passed[7] by perspiration, what quantity of it was turned into nourishment, and how much went away by the other channels and

---

1 hung upon me: 病在身上，同背着沉重的东西一样，所以用hang这字。
2 applied myself: employed myself diligently.
3 in a manner: in some sense 可以说（这种用法，现在已经不通行了）。

新登哈姆博士那篇论热病的深奥文章使我害缠绵不去的痨热病，当我看这篇好论文时候，这病老在我身上。以后我去念几位肺痨病学者的书，用这法子我得了肺病；等到最后长得太胖了，自己也有点不好意思再存这个幻想。不久又发现我自己有痛风症的各种病象，只是没有感觉到什么疼痛；可是我看一位聪明作者做的尿沙症书，就把这病医好了，他（医生平常多是医好一种，换来个别的病）把我痛风症虽然弄没有了，却给我一个胱麻病。最后我观察出好几种病在我身上综合起来；但是偶然把山克多利亚斯那本杰作拉来看一下，我决定按着我由他书里所集的那一套规则做去。学术界对这位先生的发明都知道很清楚；他为着要实行他的试验，做一种数学的椅子，精巧地安在弹簧上面，能够同一副天平似地称东西。用这样法子，他发现我们食的东西多少英两化做汗，若干分量变做滋养料，以及由

---

4 the symptoms of the gout except pain：痛风症最显明的病征是到处痛，这位先生一切病皆是个境由心造的空中楼阁，所以自己以为得了痛风症，却又感不到苦痛，把自己也弄得莫明〔名〕其妙了。

5 at length: at last.

6 the learned world：the learned people 学术界。

7 passed：disappeared or vanished 消灭。

distributions of nature.

"Having provided myself with this chair, I used to study, eat, drink, and sleep in it; insomuch that I may be said, for these three last years, to have lived in a pair of scales. I compute myself, when I am in full health, to be precisely two hundred weight, falling short of it[1] about a pound after a day's fast, and exceeding it as much after a very full meal; so that it is my continual employment to trim[2] the balance between these two volatile pounds[3] in my constitution. In my ordinary meals I fetch myself up[4] to two hundred weight and half a pound; and if after having dined I find myself fall short of it, I drink just so much small beer[5], or eat such a quantity of bread, as insufficient to make me weight. In my greatest excesses I do not transgress more than the other halfpound; which, for my health's sake, I do the first Monday in every month. As soon as I find myself duly poised after dinner, I walk till I have perspired five ounces and four scruples; and when I discover, by my chair, that I am so far reduced, I fall to[6] my books, and study away three ounces more. As for the remaining parts of the pound, I keep no account of them.[7] I do not dine and sup by the clock, but by my chair; for when that

---

1 falling short of it: failing to attain it.
2 to trim: to adjust 调节。
3 these two volatile pounds: 指吃饱时的201磅以及饿一天后的199磅这两个数目。

人身别的天然机〔器〕官用去的有多少。

"我自己预备了这么一个椅子，常常坐在上面读书，吃东西，喝水，睡觉；简直可以说最近三年中我在一副天平内过活。当我最健康的时候，我的体重刚好二百磅，饿了一天减去一磅左右，饱饱地吃了一顿后，也可以增加这么多；所以我每天都在想法怎样把我身体的二个常变磅数目弄成平均。通常每顿我要把自己做得二百零半磅；若使吃完了，我看数目不够，我就喝这么多弱麦酒或者吃这么多面包，使我刚好达到那数目。我吃得最多时候，也没有超过再一个半磅以外；为我的健康起见，每月头一个礼拜一我大吃一回，每天餐后，当我轻重合式时候，我走动一下，等到发汗减轻去五英两八十厘；由我的椅子我知道轻了这么多时候，我就开始念书，再念轻三英两。至于剩下那几英两的用处，我没有计算。我饮食起居不是照钟点，是按这椅子定的；它指示出我那磅食品用完了，我就以为自己是饿

---

4 fetch myself up：bring myself up 使我的体重达到……。
5 small beer: weak beer.
6 fall to: begin to work, or begin to read.
7 keep no account of them: do not reckon them.

informs me my pound of food is exhausted, I conclude myself to be hungry, and lay in[1] another with all diligence[2]. In my days of abstinence I lose a pound and a half, and on solemn fasts am two pounds lighter than on other days in the year.

"I allow myself, one night with another, a quarter of a pound of sleep within a few grains, more or less; and if upon my rising I find that I have not consumed my whole quantity, I take out the rest in my chair. Up an exact calculation of what I expended and received[3] the last year, which I always register in a book, I find the medium to be two hundred weight, so that I cannot discover that I am impaired one ounce in my health during a whole twelvemonth. And yet, Sir, notwithstanding this my great care to ballast myself[4] equally every day, and to keep my body in its proper poise, so it is, that I find myself in a sick and languishing condition. My complexion is grown very sallow, my pulse low, and my body hydropical. Let me therefore beg you, Sir, to consider me as your patient, and to give me more certain rules to walk by[5] than those I have already observed, and you will very much oblige.

Your humble Servant."

This letter puts me in mind of an Italian epitaph written on the monument of a Valetudinarian; *Stavo ben; ma, per star meglio, sto*

---

1 lay in: provide oneself with stock of 存一顿饭在肚里。

了，赶紧再吃下一顿。我节戒时候，失去半磅体重，严重的斋日，我比一年中别的日子轻了两磅。

"每晚我让自己睡觉里消耗去四英两左右；若使起来时，还没有消耗去那限定的数量，我就在椅上休息。将去年我身体的收入同消费仔细算一下，这些数目我总在一个本子记着，我找出总平均是二百磅，所以整年中我的健康不能说有一英两的损失。但是，先生，虽然我费很大劲使我天天都在同样的状况中，保持我身体合宜的重量，现在我却是病恹恹无精打彩〔采〕。脸孔渐渐变得非常憔悴，脉搏低微，身体也水肿起来了。先生，所以请你把我当做你的病人，给我比我已经按照做的更清楚明白的规则，使我有所依从，那么我一定非常感谢你。

你的恭敬的仆人。"

这封信使我记起一个虚弱者的墓碑上刻有一篇意大利语的

---

2 with all diligence: very diligently.
3 what I expended and received：我身体所消耗的和我所吃进去的。
4 to ballast myself: to steady myself.
5 to walk by：to live in a specified way 用种特别方法来养生。

qui[1]: which it is impossible to translate. The fear of death often proves mortal, and sets people on methods to save their lives which infallibly destroy them. This is a reflexion made by some historian[2], upon observing that there are many more thousands killed in a flight than a battle; and may be applied to those multitudes of imaginary sick persons that break their constitutions[3] by physic, and throw themselves into the arms of death, by endeavouring to escape it. This method is not only dangerous, but below the practice of a reasonable creature. To consult the preservation of life as the only end of it, to make our health our business, to engage in no action that is not part of a regimen or course of physic, are purposes so abject, so mean, so unworthy human nature, that a generous soul would rather die than submit to them. Besides that a continual anxiety for life vitiates all the relishes of it, and casts a gloom over the whole face of nature, it is impossible we should take delight in anything that we are every moment afraid of losing.

---

1 *Stavo ben*; *ma, per star meglio, sto qui*: "I was well; I would be better; and here I am."——Morley：这是讥笑那班自夸会养生的人，埋到墓里还觉得他的身体可以渐渐滋养好起来。

2 some historian：大概是指 Montaigne（虽然他不是个历史家，而是小品文学的始祖），因为他有一篇小品说起过这件事。凡是爱念小品文者，看起 Montaigne 来，一定会舍不得放下，因为他那种优柔清淡的文体，锐敏通达的心灵，使他的小品成为后世一切小品的模范。凡是做小品文章的题材，差不多逃不出他那一百多篇，一千多页之外。英译本是 Florio

墓志："以前我身体是很好,将来还要好些,现在却是这样子,"这句话是不能移译的。对于死的恐惧常常可以致命,人们怕死,找法子来救命,这法子倒一些不错地把他们害死。这是一位历史家的感想,当他看到逃走死的比打仗死的还要多几千;这也可以用于那班自己想是有病的人们,他们吃药太多,身体弄坏,为的要努力躲开死,反自己丢到死的手臂中去。这种法子不仅仅是危险的,而且是理性的动物所不应该做的。只研究怎样保存生命好像是人生唯一的目的,将保护我们的健康当作毕生的事业,除开养生吃药外什么也不干,这类意思是这样颓衰下流,有玷人性,所以心灵伟大的人宁其愿意死,不甘俯受这类思想的支配。不只对于生命不断的焦虑会将生命一切的滋味损坏净尽,将一层凄惨景象盖在自然的脸孔上,而且在我们时时刻刻只怕丢去的事物上,我们绝对不能够感到快乐。

翻的,文字太古;Cotton译本也不甚高明;最近牛津大学出版部有一种E. J. Trechmann译的,达雅两条件俱备,至于信与否,则原文是十六世纪的法文,我连拿来对照看,都没有这勇气。但是劝凡爱读小品文字的人,买一本来看看;因为虽然过了四五百年,他仍然是往古来今做小品文的第一妙手。

  3 break their constitution:伤坏他们的身体。

I do not mean, by what I have here said, that I think any one to blame[1] for taking due care of their health. On the contrary, as cheerfulness of mind and capacity for business are in a great measure[2] the effects of a well tempered constitution, a man cannot be at too much pains to cultivate and preserve it. But this care, which we are prompted to not only by common sense but by duty and instinct, should never engage us in groundless fears, melancholy apprehensions, and imaginary distempers, which are natural to every man who is more anxious to live than how to live. In short, the preservation of life should be only a secondary concern, and the direction of it our principle. If we have this frame of mind[3], we shall take the best means to preserve life, without being over solicitous about the event; and shall arrive at that point of felicity which Martial has mentioned as the perfection of happiness, of neither fearing nor wishing for death.

In answer to the gentleman, who tempers[4] his health by ounces and by scruples, and, instead of complying with those natural solicitation of hunger and thirst, drowsiness or love of exercise, governs himself by the prescriptions of his chair, I shall tell him a short fable. Jupiter[5], says the mythologist, to reward the piety of a certain countryman, promised to give him whatever he would ask.

---

1 to blame: to deserve censure.

我前面讲的话的意思并不是凡对健康有相当小心的人们是该责备的。并且，心情的愉快同作事的能力多半是良好身体的结果，因此一个人对于身体的培养保全不会有太小心。但是这种小心既不单单出于常识，而是给责任同本能所激起的，所以不要把我们带到有无根的恐惧、愁闷的杞忧同幻想的疾病，这几种弱点凡是只留心活着，不注意怎么活着的人自然会有的。总而言之，生命的保存应该是第二种重要的事，生活的处理当做最重要的事。我们若使有了这种心境，我们要尽力来保存生命，同时不可对它过于关心；这样就可达到马取鲁所谓幸福最完满的快乐境地，就是既不怕死，也不希望死的来临。

至于这位用英两英厘来调剂健康的人，他不顺从饥渴，疲倦思睡同爱运动这些天然的刺激，而受椅子的号令来管理自己，我要说个简短的寓言来回答他。神话家说天帝为要赏一个乡下人的虔敬，允许给他所想要的东西，随便什么都行。这乡下人

---

2 in a great measure: mainly.
3 this frame of mind：this mental state 这种心境。
4 tempers：调节。
5 Jupiter：希腊神话中的天上皇帝。

The countryman desired[1] that he might have the management of the weather in his own estate. He obtained his request, and immediately distributed rain, snow, and sunshine, among his several fields, as he thought the nature of the soil required. At the end of the year, when he expected to see more than ordinary crop, his harvest fell infinitely short of that of his neighbours: upon which, (says the fable,) he desired Jupiter to take the weather again into his own hands, or that otherwise he should utterly ruin himself.

---

1 desired: requested.

请求在他自己的土地内能够管理天气。他得到他所求的，立刻照他以为土地所需要的，将雨雪太阳分给他各处的田地。年底到了，他正希望他能够收获得比平常更多，他的收成却反比他的邻人都要差得非常多：于是（寓言上面这样说）他请求天帝仍然把天气收回到手中去管理，不然，他会把他自己弄得倾家荡产哩。

Oliver Goldsmith
(1728—1774)

The Man in Black

Though fond of many acquaintances[1], I desire an intimacy[2] only with a few. The Man in Black, whom I have often mentioned[3], is one whose friendship I could wish to acquire, because he possesses my esteem. His manners, it is true, are tinctured with some strange inconsistencies[4]; and he may be justly termed an humorist[5] in a nation

---

1 acquaintances: 只有"相识"的意思,不过泛泛之交。
2 intimacy: 却是很接近很亲热的了。
3 whom I have often mentioned: 这篇小品是 Goldsmith 所著《世界公民》(*The Citizen of the World*) 里面的一篇。Goldsmith 假设一个住在英国的中国人 Lien Chi Altangi 写给他的先生,中国北京礼院院长 Fum Hoam 的许多书信。因为 Lien Chi Altangi 邀游天下,四海为家,所以这部信札集叫做《世界公民》。他这种办法是模仿法国 Montesquieu (孟德斯鸠) 的《波斯通信》(*Les Lettres persanes*)。借一个外国游历人的口气,来讥讽英国的习俗,同时赞美东方的文化,外国人说英国国情,自然难免有许多笑话,所以在冷静批评里,又充满了诙谐的空气,再加上些事实做通信的线索,描写几位奇奇怪怪的人物,点缀在中间,读起来倒觉得非常有趣。当拳匪乱后 Lowes Dickinson 出版了一本《一位中国官的信》(*Letters from a Chinese Official*) 也是用这种法子来骂英国文化的缺点,而替中国人辩护的。

黑　衣　人

我虽然爱和人们认识，却只愿意同几个人弄得很熟。我常常说的那位黑衣人是个我喜欢同他做朋友的人，因为我很钦重他的人格。真的，他的态度沾染些奇怪的矛盾色彩；他可以说是以举动滑稽出名的人民里一个举动算得滑稽的人。

做小品文字的人最要紧的是观察点（the point of view），无论什么事情，只要从个新观察点看去，一定可以发见许多新的意思，除去不少从前的偏见，找到无数看了足以发噱的地方。所以做小品文字的人装老，装单身汉，装做外国人，装穷，装傻，无非是想多懂些事情的各方面。近代小品文作家 Arthur Christopher Benson 在他的杰作 *From the College Window* 的第一篇里就说 the point of view，实在是精研小品文学的神髓。许多人都以为 *The Vicar of Wakefield* 是 Goldsmith 的杰作（masterpiece），但是近来批评家却倾向于把《世界公民》当作他最成功的作品。

4 his manners...with some strange inconsistencies：这篇所描写的"黑衣人"就是 Goldsmith 自己的人格，要知道 Goldsmith 的慷慨仁爱的事情，最好阅读 Washington Irving 所做的 *Life of Goldsmith*————本比小说还要有趣味的传记。

5 humorist：有两种解释，一是"言谈诙谐的人"，一是"行为希奇，一举一动都会叫人捧腹的人"，此处作第二个意思解。不过这种说法，现在人都不大用它，但在十八世纪却常常有这样的用法。

of humorists. Though he is generous even to profusion[1], he affects[2] to be thought a prodigy[3] of parsimony and prudence; though his conversation be replete with the most sordid and selfish maxims, his heart is dilated with the most unbounded love I have known him profess himself a man-hater, while his cheek was glowing with compassion; and, while his looks were softened into pity, I have heard him use the language of the most unbounded ill-nature. Some affect humanity and tenderness, others boast of having such dispositions from Nature; but he is the only man I ever knew who seemed ashamed of his natural benevolence[4]. He takes as much pains to hide

---

1　generous even to profusion：慷慨太过，简直变做浪费。

2　affects：pretends to be假装。

3　prodigy：person who is a wonderful example of some quality奇人。

4　who seemed... natural benevolence：在《世界公民》中有一封信，说明黑衣人为什么会有这种七古八怪的性格。那书里叙述的，多半同Goldsmith生平相仿佛。黑衣人的父亲是一个小牧师，收入虽然不多，但为人极慷慨，于是有一班穷亲友，天天靠他吃饭；他觉得学问品格是真值得贵重的东西，金钱是身外之物，无足重轻，所以他平日只教他儿子应当怎样帮助人，怎地急公好义，却没有替他儿子打算个谋生之道，这老头子死了，给他儿子只是个空空洞洞临死时的祝福。那时这位黑衣人才二十二岁，只好出去问世；他以为结交了好多朋友，一定到处可以得到帮助。起先有人劝他当牧师，他觉得当牧师要穿上那小孩子似的衣服，无聊得很，不愿意干。就依附在一个王公大臣的门下，可是他生性真不会阿谀谄媚，王公大臣嫌他无用，因而就摈之门外了。他碰了这个钉子，以后便想在爱情里找些安慰，他向一个他平时以为对他有好意的女子求婚，女子说很愿意嫁他，可是她三月前已经嫁给他的情敌了，劝他去向她那又老又丑的姑

虽然他慷慨到像浪费，他在人前却假装是个鄙吝鬼；不管他说多少顶下流自私自利的话，他的心是满涨了无限的爱。我看过他自认是个人类的厌恶者，当时他的脸却因为同情于人们红得发烧；他面容现出怜悯柔情的时节，我听他口里却说癖〔脾〕气顶坏的人所说的话。有人假装仁爱，人道的样子，还有自夸生来具有这副柔软心肠的；他倒是我所看见唯一的人，会好像

母求婚，大概总有成功的希望。他万分失望，想去找朋友们帮忙，他从前不是有许多朋友都说愿意帮助他的吗？有一位在城里当书记，从前老说要借钱给他——当黑衣人有钱的时候。现在他跑去借钱，却当面受了他一番教训，并且说，没有钱，来借债的人，将来一定没有钱还债的。他气极了，就到一个他自以为是最知己的朋友处去和他商量，同样地受了一番教训之后，问他要借多少，他说要用三百镑，打算向他借二百镑，其余向另一个朋友想法子。于是这位最知己朋友劝他，不如一起都向那位朋友借去，到〔倒〕是件省事的办法。他在这穷困不堪的时节，还替一位朋友作保，后来朋友逃了，因而他被抓去关在牢狱里。他高兴得不得，以为关在牢狱里的人，既都是人生路上的失败者，自然全是老实忠厚，不然怎么会同他一样地来受这铁窗的风味呢？可是，牢狱里人同外面一样，势争力夺，世态炎凉，比外面简直更利害。他出狱后，还是昏天糊地过着日子，忽然一天遇见他从前一个老朋友，这位朋友非常愚蠢，然而俭朴勤谨居然成家立业，做起官来了。他忽然悟到要想扶助旁人，非自己先能自立不可(The true way of being able to relieve others was first to aim at in dependence myself.)，他立刻改弦更辙，勤俭起来，不到几年，他也成了个在社会上有地位的绅士了。他虽然饱经世故，尝尽人生的苦楚，看破人们的虚伪，但是他仍然是慈爱为怀，所以有这样奇怪的言行之不一致。Samuel Johnson说，Goldsmith说起话来，是位智者，做出的事，却是傻子。这是Goldsmith的毛病，也就是他人格上最可爱的地方。

his feelings, as any hypocrite would to conceal his indifference; but on every unguarded[1] moment the mask drops off, and reveals him to the most superficial observer.

In one of our late excursions into the country, happening to discourse upon the provision that was made for the poor in England, he seemed amazed how any of his countrymen could be so foolishly weak as to relieve occasional objects of charity[2], when the laws had made such ample provision for their support. "In every parish-house," says he, "the poor are supplied with food, clothes, fire, and a bed to lie on; they want no more, I desire no more myself; yet still they seem discontented. I'm surprised at the inactivity of our magistrates in not taking up[3] such vagrants, who are only a weight[4] upon the industrious; I'm surprised that the people are found to relieve them, when they must be at the same time sensible that it, in some measure[5], encourages idleness, extravagance, and imposture. Were I to advise any man for whom I had the least regard, I would caution him by all means[6] not to be imposed upon by their false pretences; let me assure you, Sir, they are impostors, every one of them; and rather merit[7] a prison than relief."

---

1 unguarded: careless.
2 objects of charity: 慈善的对象（就是可怜人）。
3 taking up: arresting or taking into custody 抓来。
4 weight: burden.

对自己天然的慈心觉得害羞。他遮盖这情感的努力不下于那班伪君子存起本来冷心肠的费劲；可是在不留心时，他这假面具丢下来了，就是最糊涂的人也会看出他的真相。

在近来到乡间的旅行里，有一次我们偶然谈起英国对贫民的救济，他好像很惊奇为什么竟有人会心地柔弱地呆到去救济那路上碰着的可怜人，因为法律替他们的生活既然供给得这么完备了。他说，"在每个区立穷人院里，穷人都有衣，食，火同睡的床铺供给得很完全；他们不至于有什么别的缺乏，就是我自己也不想要什么旁的东西；但是他们好像还没有满意。我真奇怪为什么长官不管他们，不把这班连累勤作者的游荡汉关起；我还奇怪天下找得出去赒济他们的人们，因为人们同时心里一定会明白，这样干有些像鼓舞人去懒惰，浪费同做假。若使叫我去对一个我稍稍有点关心的人说，我一定劝他千万留心不要给他们的假理由哄住；先生，请相信我的话，他们全是骗人的，他们值得闭在监狱里，不合受我们的援助。"

5　in some measure: partly.
6　by all means: certainly; undoubtedly.
7　merit: deserve.

He was procceding in this strain[1] earnestly, to dissuade me from an inprudence of which I am seldom guilty, when an old man, who still had about him the remnants of tattered finery[2], implored our compassion. He assured us that he was no common beggar, but forced into the shameful profession to support a dying wife and five hungry children. Being prepossessed against such falsehoods, his story had not the least influence upon me; but it was quite otherwise with the Man in Black; I could see it visibly operate[3] upon his countenance, and effectually interrupt his harangue. I could easily perceive that his heart burned[4] to relieve the five starving children, but he seemed ashamed to me. While he thus hesitated between compassion and pride[5], I pretended to look another way, and he seized this opportunity[6] of giving the poor petitioner a piece of silver, bidding him at the same time, in order that I should hear, go work for his bread, and not tease passengers with such impertinent falsehoods for the future.

As he had fancied himself quite unperceived, he continued, as we proceeded, to rail against beggars with as much animosity as before; he threw in[7] some episodes on his own amazing prudence

---

1 strain: manner or way.
2 tattered finery: 可见这个乞丐是个穷困无以聊生的浪子，所以还穿着烂破的锦绣衣服，下面所说甚多，为妻子故才出此下策，自然是句谎言。
3 operate: produce a certain effeet 使他的脸变色，现出苦恼的样子。

他正要这样地继续往下说，严肃地劝我不要犯那我实在不常犯的毛病，一个老人身上还有破烂的绸衣碎块挂着来求我们的怜悯。他要我们相信他不是普通的叫化子，他为着要养活一个将死的老婆同五个饥饿的孩子，逼到干这可耻的生涯。我对这类假话，心里早不相信，他的话不能感动我；但是这套话对黑衣人的影响就大不相同了；我看出他脸孔发生变化，最后这故事打断他那滔滔不绝的演说。我很容易看出他心中热烈地想救济这五个饥饿的小孩，但他不好意思在我面前显出他的弱点。当他的同情和自尊两种情绪相冲突，犹疑未决的时候，我故意向别方看，他就乘这机会给了这可怜求乞人一块银洋，同时为着说给我听，他故意叫他去工作谋食，不要再拿这无聊的大谎和走路人麻烦。

他以为我一点都没有看见，所以我们走时，他还继续同起先一样忿怒万分地骂叫化子；他插说些自己惊人的谨慎同俭啬

---

4 burned：was very eager 热心。
5 pride：有好坏二方面，可以作"骄傲"，也可以作"自尊"解，此处当从第二义。
6 seized this opportunity：抓着这个机会。
7 threw in：inserted 加说些。

and economy, with his profound skill in discovering impostors, he explained the manner in which he would deal with beggars, were he a magistrate , hinted at enlarging some of the prisons for their reception, and told two stories of ladies that were robbed by beggar-men. He was beginning third to the same purpose[1], when a sailor with a wooden leg once more crossed our walks, desiring our pity, and blessing our limbs[2]. I was for going on[3] without taking any notice, but my friend, looking wistfully upon the poor petitioner, bade me stop, and he would show me with how much ease he could at any time detect an impostor.

He now, therefore, assumed a look of importance[4], and in an angry tone began to examine the sailor, demanding in what engagement he was thus disabled and rendered unfit for service. The sailor replied in a tone as angrily as he, that he had been an officer on board a private ship of war, and that he had lost his leg abroad, in defence of those who did nothing at home. At this reply, all my friend's importance vanished in a moment; he had not a single question more to ask; he now only studied[5] what method he should take to relieve him unobserved. He had, however, no easy part[6] to act,

---

 1 to the same purpose: serving to illustrate the same idea.
 2 blessing our limbs: 水手自己靠着木脚行走，赞美那班两脚健全的人。
 3 for going on: for 有"赞成，主张"的意思，这个 phrase 作"我是打算往前走"解。

的故事，和他点破装假的大本领；他解释若使他做了长官，他对叫化子的办法是怎么样，露出他要扩张监狱来收容他们的意思，告诉我两件乞丐抢妇女东西的故事。他刚要说第三样相同的故事，一个用木腿走路的水手又走到我们面前，希望能够得我们的怜悯，祝福我们两腿的健康。我打算走过去不睬他，但是我这朋友仔细地看这可怜求乞人，请我站住，说他要我看他多么容易无论什么时候都能揭穿这类欺骗者。

所以他用一种严重的脸孔，不高兴的声音开始盘问这水手，问他是为了干什么事弄得这般躯体残缺，不能再执行他的职务。那水手也同样含着怒气地答道，他从前在战舰上做军官，为保护这班在家里没事干的人，在外面打仗把腿打坏了。听这话，我朋友的那种傲慢态度立刻完全消灭了；他没有话再问；他现在只研究他用什么法子能够偷偷地赒济这水手。这事倒不大好

---

4 a look of importance：a serious look 严重的面孔。
5 studied: considered attentively.
6 part: share of work or work.

as he was obliged to preserve the appearance of ill-nature before me, and yet relieve himself by relieving the sailor. Casting, therefore, a furious look upon some bundles of chips which the fellow carried in a string at his back, my friend demanded how he sold his matches; but not waiting for a reply, desired in a surly tone to have a shilling's worth[1]. The sailor seemed at first surprised at his demand, but soon recollecting himself[2], and presenting his whole bundle—"Here, master," says he, "take all my cargo, and blessing into the bargain[3]."

It is impossible to describe with what an air[4] of triumph my friend marched off with his new purchase; he assured me that he was firmly of opinion that those fellows must have stolen their goods who could thus afford to sell them for half value. He informed me of several different uses to which those chips might be applied: he expatiated largely[5] upon the savings that would result from lighting candles with a match instead of thrusting them into the fire. He averred that he would as soon have parted with a tooth as his money to those vagabonds, unless for some valuable consideration[6]. I

---

1 desired in a surly tone to have a shiling's worth: 火柴是非常贱的东西，几个辨士就可以买许多，自然用不到花一先令来买，而且在十八世纪先令的价值比现在为贵；所以几包火柴用一先令来买，就是等于给他一个先令。

2 recollecting himself: 水手起先不明白黑衣人的动机，后来镇静一想，才知道他故意以买火柴来掩盖这慈善的行为。

办,因为他不得不在我面前保持那坏癖子的面孔,却又要设法去救济这水手来救济他自己心中的苦痛。所以对这个人挂在背后,绳子穿着的几包火柴凶凶地望了一眼,我这朋友问他的火柴卖什么价钱;不等他回答,声音粗暴地向他要一先令的火柴。水手起初对他的话好像有些惊奇,一会儿心里明白,将所有火柴都给他,口里说:"先生,请将我所有的货都拿去,此外我还送你一个祝福。"

我这朋友带着这新买的东西〔往〕望前走,那种得意神气是描写不出的。他对我说他坚决相信肯以半价出售东西的人,他的东西一定是偷来的。他告诉我这种火柴各种不同的用处;还说一阵用火柴燃洋蜡比将洋蜡拿到火炉里点会多么节省洋蜡。他用劲地说,若使没有什么对他便宜的地方,他绝不会拿钱给这班流氓,同他不至于拔下牙齿送给他们一样。我不知道他这

---

3 into the bargain: over and above what is stipulated or in addition.
4 air:态度,神情。
5 largely: freely or a great deal.
6 some valuable consideration:"打起算盘来,觉得我自己占了便宜"的意思。

cannot tell how long this panegyric upon frugality and matches might have continued, had not his attention been called off by another object more distressful than either of the former. A woman in rags, with one child in her arms, and another on her back, was attempting to sing ballads[1], but with such a mournful voice that it was difficult to determine whether she was singing or crying. A wretch who in the deepest distress still aimed at good-humour, was an object my friend was by no means[2] capable of withstanding[3]: his vivacity and his discourse were intantly interrupted; upon this occasion his very dissimulation[4] had forsaken him. Even in my presence, he immediately applied[5] his hands to his pockets, in order to relieve her; but guess his confusion when he found he had already given away all the money he carried about his to former objects. The misery painted in the woman's visage was not half so strongly expressed as the agony[6] in his. He continued to search for some time, but to no purpose[7], till, at length, recollecting himself, with a face of ineffable good nature, as he had no money, he put into her hands his shilling's worth of matches.

---

  1 to sing ballads: 英国穷女人常在街角屋旁，唱着歌谣小调，向行人要钱，有时还奏弹手提琴和着。
  2 by no means: certainly not; on no account whatever.
  3 withstanding: 看着忍不住（慈悲之心油然而生）。
  4 his very dissimulation: 这个very是加重语气用的。

对俭啬同火柴的赞美要往下说多久,若使他的注意不转到一个比前面二个更悲惨的情形上去。一个衣服褴褛的妇人,手里抱个小孩,后面背一个,勉强地唱些小调求乞,她的声调是这么凄凉的,听的人分不出是唱还是哭。一个可怜人在深深的苦痛里,却要强为欢笑,这情境我的朋友绝对忍耐不下:他的高兴同谈话即刻停住了;这回他也忘记去扮假面目了。甚至于当我面前,他立刻伸手到衣袋里去掏钱来救助她;当他发现他带在身边的钱已经完全给从前两个了,读者,你猜一猜他那时焦急的样子。那女人脸上现的哀容赶不上他面上苦恼的一半。他继续掏了好几次,都没有达到目的,等到最后他自己记起,用种说不出的和蔼态度,他将他那值得一先令的火柴送到她手里。

---

5 applied: put.
6 agony:是非常利害的苦痛,比 pain 和 misery 都重些。
7 to no purpose: in vain 没有结果。

Charles Lamb

(1775—1834)

Detached[1] Thoughts on Books and Reading

To mind the inside of a book is to entertain one's self with the forced product of another man's brain. Now I think a man of quality[2] and breeding may be much amused with the natural sprouts of his own.

—Lord Foppington[3] in *Relapse*[4]

An ingenious acquaintance of my own was so much struck[5] with this bright sally[6] of his Lordship, that he has left off reading altogether, to the great improvement of his originality. At the hazard of

---

1 detached: desultory.
2 a man of quality: one of the upper classes.
3 Lord Foppington：剧里一个人物。
4 *The Relapse*：十八世纪喜剧家 Sir John Vanbrugh 编的一本剧本的名字。

读 书 杂 感

  去注意一本书的内容是拿别人脑里榨出的东西来消遣，我却想一个受过良好教育的上等社会人对自己脑里自由地涌出的思想会觉得非常好玩。

    ——《重蹈覆辙》剧中福宾汤爵士说的话

  爵士大人这句漂亮的机锋是这么深深地打进了我一个朋友的心坎里，他已经完全不念书，因此他脑里天外飞来的簇新思想大有增加。不管我有没有失去我思想出奇的令名的危险，我

---

 5 was...struck: was...impressed.
 6 sally：冲口而出的妙语（所以意译为"机锋"，但实在并不含有讥讽的意思）。

losing some credit on this head, I must confess that I dedicate no inconsiderable portion of my time to other people's thoughts. I dream away my life in others's peculations. I love to lose myself in other men's minds. When I am not walking, I am reading; I cannot sit and think. Books think for me.

I have no repugnances. Shaftesbury[1] is not too genteel for me, nor *Jonathan Wild*[2] too low. I can read anything which I call a book. There are things in that shape which I cannot allow for such.

In this catalogue of books *which are no books—biblia a-biblia*—I reckon Court Calendars, Directories, Pocket Books(the Literary excepted), Draught Boards, bound and lettered at the back, Scientific Treatises, Almanacks, Statutes at Large; the works of Hume[3], Gibbon[4], Robertson[5], Beattie[6], Soame Jenyns[7], and, generally, all those volumes which "no gentleman's library should be without"[8];

---

1 Shaftesbury：十七世纪一位散文作家，著有许多关于伦理的著作，他的文体优柔雅驯是其长处，读起来音调铿锵，但有时失之无气魄，句子太长。

2 *Jonathan Wild*：十八世纪小说家Fielding著的小说，叙述一个流氓由他出世到上绞台的历史，全书描写堕落生活，形容入微，使人看着仿佛有一担阴郁之气，压在身上，但是于性格的描写，确是入木三分，作者气魄之大，任何读者都会佩服。

3 Hume：十八世纪的一个哲学家，历史家兼小品文家，文笔比较枯燥些。

总要自己承认我供献不少的时间，去念旁人的思想。在别人的空想里，我做梦地度去我的时光。我喜欢将自己沉溺在旁人的心灵里。我不走路的时候，就得念书；我不能坐着苦想。书籍替我想一切的东西。

我对书籍没有什么厌恶。沙弗斯伯利的文章，我不觉得太细腻优柔，《朱黎山·王尔德》的我也不以为太下流。凡是我认做是书的，我都能念。有的带着书的外形，我却不能当做是书。

在这《不是书的书》目录里，我可以数出宫庭起居注指南，袖珍书本（文学的除外），装订好而背后写着字的棋盘，科学论文，历书，法典大全；休谟，吉朋，鲁百孙，必提，孙安·金立斯的著作，以及一切所谓"绅士家里书库不可不备的书"；同

---

4 Gibbon：十八世纪的一个历史家，他的《罗马衰亡史》（*Decline and Fall of the Roman Empire*）是一部不朽的杰作，他的文体雄丽壮伟，辞句波澜起伏，为一代文宗。Macaulay 文体半得之于 Gibbon。但 Lamb 好清新秀逸或巧思奇构之作，如 Walton，Browne，Burton 等之书，故不喜 Gibbon。

5 Robertson：十八世纪的一个历史家。

6 Beattie：十八世纪的一个诗人。

7 Soame Jenyns：十八世纪的一个历史家。

8 "no gentleman's library should be without"：这是书店做广告时用的话。

the Histories of Flavius Josephus[1] (that learned Jew), and Paley's[2] Moral Philosophy. With these exceptions, I can read almost anything. I bless my stars[3] for a taste so catholic, so unexcluding.

I confess that it moves my spleen[4] to see these *things in book's clothing* perched upon shelves, like false saints, usurpers of true shrines, intruders into the sanctuary, thrusting out the legitimate occupants. To reach down[5] a well-bound semblance of a volume, and hope it some kind-hearted play-book, then, opening what "seem its leaves," to come bolt[6] upon a withering *Population Essay*[7]. To expect a Steele[8], or a Farquhar[9], and find—Adam Smith[10]. To view a well-arranged assortment of blockheaded Encyclopaedias (Anglicanas or Metropolitanas[11])set out in an array of Russia or Morocco[12], when a tithe[13] of that good leather would comfortably

---

1 Flavius Josephus：一世纪的一个犹太历史家。

2 Paley：十八世纪的一个哲学家兼政治学家。

3 I bless my stars：英人相信，小孩生下时候，天上所照的什么星与他一生的性情命运都有关系。如生时带 Mercury（水星），则性情活泼，带 Saturn（木星），则沉郁愁闷等等。所以一个人赋性快乐，我们说他 mercurial，说天天忧虑的人是 saturnine。

4 spleen: irritability.

5 to reach down: to take down.

6 come bolt: come suddenly.

7 a withering *Population Essay*：一本憔悴凋残的《人口论》(《人口论》是说人口的繁殖学说，上面却加上 withering 这形容字，字面的意思是那本书破烂得很利害，但是这字却与人口的繁殖这字相对，所以是双关意)。

福利非亚斯·朱西发斯（那位博学的犹太人）的历史，伯黎的伦理学。这些除开之外，我差不多什么东西都可以念。我的趣味能够这么广大并包，我真要庆祝自己。

看这类"穿着书的外衣的东西"栖止在书架上，像假圣人，霸占真正神龛者，侵犯神殿者，反把正当要排在上面的赶了出来，我自认这件事使我很愤怒。拿下一本装订得好像书的东西，心里希望这是个心地温和的剧本，翻开那"像书叶子"的东西，突然碰到一个憔悴凋零的《人口论》。希望得一本斯蒂鲁的文集或者沙区哈的喜剧，却遇着——亚当·斯密斯。看到那笨傻的百科全书（"大英"的或"京师"的）整部好好地排着，用俄罗斯或摩洛哥皮装饰，当那好皮的十分之一就够把我那冻得发战的大书舒服地再穿上一层外衣；使巴纳西鲁沙斯面目一新，

---

8 Steele：十八世纪的小品文家，也可以说是英国定期出版物的开山始祖。

9 Farquhar：十七世纪的喜剧家。

10 Adam Smith：十八世纪的经济学大家，《原富》的作者。

11 Anglicanas or Metropolitanas：是两部百科全书版子的名字。

12 Russia or Morocco：俄国或摩洛哥出产的皮，常用做书面。

13 tithe: a tenth.

reclothe my shivering folios; would renovate Paracelsus[1] himself, and enable old Raymund Lully[2] to look like himself again in the world. I never see these impostors, but I long[3] to strip them, to warm my ragged veterans[4] in their spoils.

To be strong-backed and neat-bound is the desideratum of a volume. Magnificence comes after[5]. This, when it can be afforded, is not to be lavished upon all kinds of books indiscriminately. I would not dress a set of Magazines, for instance, in full suit. The deshabille, or half-binding (with Russia backs ever) is our costume[6]. A Shakespeare[7], or a Milton[8](unless the first editions[9]), it were mere foppery to trick out in gay apparel. The possession of them confers no distinction. The exterior of them(the things themselves being so common[10]), strange to say, raises no sweet emotions, no tickling sense of property[11] in the owner. Thomson's *Seasons*[12], again, looks

---

1 Paracelsus: 十六世纪有名的德国点金术家，一个无所不通的大学者。Browning有一首长诗，歌咏这位以理智为中心的学者，诗之结局说出纯以理智为生命的源泉，则生活必流于空虚无味。

2 Lully: 罗马的一个哲学家。

3 long: wish.

4 veterans: 老卒（此指他的书用了几十年，面破页掉，始终依随着他，真像险苦备历的老卒）。

5 magnificence comes after: magnificence may be considered afterward.

6 our costume: Lamb这篇文章登在 *London Magazine* 上面，故用our这字。

破旧的来门·鲁立也能在世上重复旧观。我每回看这班冒充者，总想把他们的衣服剥下，将这抢来的东西盖上我那穿百结衣的老书，使能得到温暖。

有坚固的背脊，清清楚楚地订着，这是一本书不可少的条件。然后再谈到华丽。就是办得到讲究华丽，我们也不应该毫无分别地化费在一切书的上面。好像，我不情愿把一套杂志穿上整整齐齐的衣服一样。便服或者半装订（老是用俄国皮做背脊）是"我们"的装束。将一本莎士比亚或密尔敦（除非是第一版）盖上艳服，完全是纨袴〔绔〕虚荣爱慕浮华的行为。这种浓妆不能增加它们的价值。说来也奇怪，这种外表（这外表是那么普通的）不能引起快感，也不会增加书的主人占有的愉

---

7 A Shakespeare：一本 Shakespeare 的诗集。

8 a Milton：一本 Milton 诗集。

9 the first editions：第一版的莎翁集或 Milton 的作品，极不易得，所以要如是贵重。

10 the things... so common：莎翁及 Milton 的书，家传户诵，任一书肆皆有，用不着好书皮保护。

11 tickling sense of property：爱得一件东西，手痒难过，莎翁在 *Julius Caesar* 里说一个食赃的人有 an itching palm，也是这种意思。

12 Thomson's *Seasons*：Thomson 是十八世纪初叶有些浪漫派色彩的诗人，《四季》是他的杰作，中多述乡间故事，及田舍风光。

best (I maintain it) a little torn, and dog's-eared. How beautiful to a genuine lover of reading are the sullied leaves, and worn-out appearance, nay, the very odour (beyond Russia)[1], if we would not forget kind feelings in fastidiousness, of an old "Circulating Library"[2] *Tom Jones*[3], or *Vicar of Wakefield* [4]! How they speak of the thousand thumbs, that have turned over their pages with delight! —of the lone sempstress whom they may have cheered (milliner or harder-working mantua-maker) after her long day's needle-toil, running far[5] into midnight, when she has snatched an hour, ill spared from sleep, to steep[6] her cares, as in some Lethean cup[7], in spelling out their enchanting contents! Who would have them a whit less soiled? What better condition could we desire to see them in?

In some respects the better a book is, the less it demands from binding. Fielding[8], Smollett[9], Sterne[10], and all that class of perpetually

---

1 the very odour (beyond Russia): 书用得太常了，免不了有人们手汗的味。

2 "Circulating Library": "流通图书馆"（这是十八世纪才有的一种很好的组织，每人按月纳些费，可以向一个共同组织的图书馆，把书拿回来看，这样的机关对于普及教育方面很有用处）。

3 *Tom Jones*: Fielding 所著的一本小说，是他的杰作，有些批评家都承认为英国最好的小说。

4 *Vicar of Wakefield*: 这本书是 Goldsmith 做的，在中国很风行，他的妙处已经用不着说了。

5 running far: continuing far.

6 to steep: to drown.

快。还有汤姆生的《四季》这本诗集最漂亮的时候（我是这样主张的）是有些撕破处同折卷的页子。由一个真真爱念书的人看来，"流通图书馆"的老旧的《汤姆·朱黎斯》同《威克菲尔牧师传》的沾污的纸页同破烂的外表是多么美丽，而且，若使我们不因为过于讲究而忘却人类的温情，那种气味（俄国皮以外的气味），也是何等的可爱！这些破书指示出曾经有千个手指快乐地翻那页子！——有的由它们得些快乐的寂寞女缝匠（做帽带首饰的，或者勤作的做女衣者）在她长日工作之后，已经入了深夜，她由睡眠里勉强地偷出一个钟头，一字一字地拼出那迷人的内容，好像将她的烦恼浸在一杯忘川的水里头！谁愿意这些书少有些污点？我们能够希望它们有什么更好的形相吗？

越是好的书，仿佛越不需要精美的装订。菲鲁丁，斯姆立，

---

7 Lethean cup：希腊神话，在阴间有一条河，名做Lethe，那河里的水人吃了可以忘却前生一切的事情，所以Lethean cup可以当作"忘忧水"解。

8 Fielding：十八世纪大小说家。

9 Smollett：十八世纪大小说家，著有 *Humphry Clinkers*。

10 Sterne：十八世纪大小说家，著有 *Tristram Shandy*，*Sentimental Journey*。

self-reproductive volumes—Great Nature's Stereo-types—we see them individually perish with less regret, because we know the copies of them to be"eterne". But where a book is at once both good and rare —where the individual is almost the species, and when that perishes,
We know not where is that Promethean torch[1]
That can its light relumine—
Such a book, for instance, as the *Life of the Duke of Newcastle*, by his Duchess[2]—no casket is rich enough, no casing sufficiently durable, to honour and keep safe such a jewel.

Not only rare volumes of this description, which seem hopeless ever to be reprinted; but old editions of writers, such as Sir Philip Sydney[3], Bishop Taylor[4], Milton in his prose-works[5], Fuller[6]—of whom we have reprints, yet the books themselves, though they go about[7], and are talked of here and there, we know, have not endeni-

---

1 Promethean torch：Prometheus是天上的一个神祇，他为着要帮助人们，从天上偷取了天火，用火把燃着带到地上来，给了他们，但这事后来天帝（Jupiter）晓得了，于是非常生怒，把他绑在高加索山（Mount Caucasus）上，每日叫鹰啄食他的心肝，还叫许多鬼来磨难他。希腊诗人Aeschylus著有*Prometheus Unbound*《Prometheus的解放》一篇悲剧。及至浪漫派极盛时代，把Prometheus当作替人类争自由，和抵抗运命的神，将Prometheus的火象征地解释做人类智慧的源泉，因此对Prometheus赞美备至，最有名的是Shelley的*Prometheus Unbound*一首长诗。

2 His Duchess：the Duchess of Newcastle做的《新堡公爵传》，是Lamb爱读的一本书。

3 Sir Philip Sydney：英国十六世纪的诗人，他欢喜歌咏牧羊生活，还

斯东,同一切这一类自己老是生下新版的书——"大自然的铅版"——我们看它们个本的销灭,没有痛心,因为我们知道这一部书是"万古不灭"的。但是一本同时又好又难得的书——差不多是海内孤本,当它毁坏了,

  我们不知道那里去找普鲁米修斯的火,

  能够将它的光重新燃起——

这种书,比方像那公爵夫人所做的《新堡公爵传》——我们来敬重,来保存这样一个宝贝,没有珍贵的匣子会说是够得上,没有套子可以算坚固得够用了。

  不止这类难得的,又没有再版希望的书值得这样看重;就是菲立·史得利,泰禄主教,做散文的密尔敦,莆禄等作家的老版子——虽然我们也有翻印本到处流通,人们有时也谈到它

做有很好的十四行诗。

 4 Bishop Taylor:英国十七世纪的神学家,他做的 *Holy Living and Holy Dying* 是和《天路历程》(Bunyan's *Pilgrim's Progress*)同样盛行于民间的书。

 5 Milton in his prose-works:Milton 的散文流传不如他的诗那样广。

 6 Fuller:英国十七世纪的传记兼历史家,文体奇妙,也是 Lamb 爱读的作家。

 7 go about: circulate.

zened themselves (nor possibly ever will) in the national heart, so as to become stock books[1]—it is good to possess these in durable and costly covers. I do not care for a First Folio of Shakespeare. You cannot make a pet book of an author whom everybody reads. I rather prefer the common editions of Rowe and Tonson[2], without notes, and with plates, which, being so execrably bad, serve as maps, or modest remembrancers, to the text; and without pretending to any supposable emulation with it, are so much better than the Shakespeare gallery engravings, which did. I have a community of feeling with my countrymen about his plays[3], and I like those editions of him best, which have been oftenest tumbled about and handled. —On the contrary, I cannot read Beaumont and Fletcher[4] but in Folio. The Octavo editions are painful to look at. I have no sympathy with them. If they were as much read as the current editions of the other poet, I should prefer them in that shape to the older one. I do not know a more heartless sight than the reprint of the *Anatomy of Melancholy*[5]. What need was there of unearthing the bones of that fantastic old great man, to expose them in a winding-sheet of the newest fashion

---

1 stock books: common books.

2 Rowe and Tonson：是印行莎翁全集的出版者。

3 I have a community of feeling with my countrymen about his plays：由这点可见 Lamb 对于人们热烈的同情。

4 Beaumont and Fletcher：莎翁同时的戏曲作家，他们二人常合编戏曲，

们，可是我们知道它们还没有（将来也未必能够）镕化在我们民族心里，所以不能变做通常的书——这类的书我们还是用坚固值钱的皮装起好些。我并不爱第一次对折版的莎士比亚。我倒喜欢雷和汤生的版本，没有注解，附上的铜版印得非常坏，只可当张地图或者提起书里说的是什么；并没有野心想和原版比赛，所以比那莎氏雕刻木版本还好得多，因为木版本是打算和原版竞争的。我对他的戏剧和国人有共通的情感，所以我爱那最常在人手里翻转的版子。——同这个相反的，堡门和弗烈取的剧本，我非对折本念不下去。八开本看起来觉得恶心，不能使我生出同情。若使这种版本的读者也有念别个诗人通行本的人那么多，那么我也可以喜欢这八开本，不再那么样爱老版了。我没有看过一个比翻印《愁闷的分析》再麻木不仁的举动。把这古老的伟大老头子骨头掘起来，用最时髦的寿衣捆着拿来给现代人骂，这又何必呢？那个不幸的老板会梦想伯敦也有受

所以有许多剧本后来分不出那一篇是谁做的。

5 *Anatomy of Melancholy*：Burton 做的。他行文光怪陆离，想入非非（fantastic），Lamb 好奇成性，所以耽读此书不厌。

to modern censure? What hapless stationer¹ could dream of Burton ever becoming popular? —The wretched Malone could not do worse, when he bribed the sexton of Stratford church to let him whitewash the painted effigy of old Shakespeare, which stood there, in rude but lively fashion depicted, to the very colour of the cheek, the eye, the eyebrow, hair, the very dress he used to wear—the only authentic testimony we had, however imperfect, of these curious parts and parcels²of him. They covered him over with a coat of white paint. By—³, if I had been a justice of peace for Warwickshire, I would have clapped both commentator and sexton fast in the stocks, for a pair of meddling sacrilegious varlets.

I think I see them at their work—these sapient trouble-tombs.

Shall I be thought fantastical, if I confess, that the names of some of our poets sound sweeter, and have a finer relish to the ear—to mine, at least—than that of Milton or of Shakespeare? It may be, that the latter are more staled and rung upon in common discourse⁴. The sweetest names, and which carry a perfume in the mention, are,

---

1 hapless stationer：意思是 Burton 的书，一定卖不出去，书店老板免不了赔本。

2 parts and parcels: an essential part.

3 By—：发誓时用的话，如 by God 等，意思是"上帝鉴之"，此处所以省去代以一横，是因为十七八世纪作家忌用粗熟之语入文，故遇有此类字常略去而代以记号。Lamb 虽然生在十九世纪，他却惯喜模仿英国古人，所以也省去这字。

大众欢迎的日子？——就是下贱的马伦也不能干件再坏的事情，马伦用钱略贿司图拉福教堂的事务员，让他进去用灰水刷白那带彩色的老莎翁雕像，那像本来站在那里很粗糙地但是栩栩如生地配上颜色，甚至面颊，眼睛，眉毛，头发，他常穿衣服一切的颜色都画出来——无论怎地不完全，这是我们所有唯一的关于莎翁奇怪形容的记载。他们用一层白垩盖上去。我指——为誓，若使我是瓦亦克州的法官，我要把他们当作一双瞎闹渎圣的无赖，用足枷将这注书家同事务员都紧紧地枷住。

他们——这班捣乱坟墓的聪明人——工作的样子，现在活现在我眼前。

我会不会被人们当做胡思乱想的人，若使我老实地说，有几位我们诗人的名字读起来特别甜蜜，听到耳里另有一种滋味——最少，对我是这样子——比密尔敦，莎士比亚都来得悦耳？或者，莎士比亚这名字在普通谈话里太常用了，弄得走味了。最甜蜜的名字，说起来带着香气的是岂·玛绿，都莱敦，何桑

---

4 the latter are more staled and rung upon in common discourse：因为这两位诗人的名字，太常说了，所以我们听不出这两个名字的妙处。

Kit Marlowe[1], Drayton[2], Drummond of Hawthornden[3], and Cowley[4].

Much depends upon when and where you read a book. In the five or six impatient minutes, before the dinner is quite ready, who would think of taking up the *Faërie Queene*[5] for a stop-gap, or a volume of Bishop Andrewes'[6] sermons?

Milton almost requires a solemn service of music to be played before you enter upon him. But he brings his music, to which, who listens, had need bring docile thoughts, and purged ears.

Winter evenings—the world shut out—with less of ceremony the gentle Shakespeare enters.[7] At such a season, the *Tempest*, or his own *Winter's Tale*—

These two poets you cannot avoid reading aloud—to yourself, or (as it chances) to some single person listening. More than one—and it degenerates into an audience.[8]

Books of quick interest, that hurry on[9] for incidents, are for the

---

1 Kit Marlowe：就是Christopher Marlowe，十六世纪诗剧家，莎翁受他的影响很大。

2 Drayton：十六世纪的英国诗人。

3 Drummond of Hawthornden：Drummond是十七世纪英国诗人，因为他住在Hawthornden，所以人家都这样叫他。

4 Cowley：十七世纪的诗人兼小品文家，他只留给我们十一篇小品，但每篇都充满着微妙的思想，清新的文句，开英国小品文学的先河。

5 *Faërie Queene*：伊利萨伯时代的诗人Edmund Spenser的作品，文字极华丽典雅的能事，但念起来极其费劲。

登的都拉门，和考莱。

读一本书，在"什么时候"同"什么地方"读，都很有关系的。在大餐没有预备好以前，剩的五六分不耐烦的时间，谁会想拿《仙后》或者一本安徒留斯主教的训语来填这一点的闲空呢?

在读密尔敦以前，你差不多要先听一套严肃的音乐才行。但是密尔敦诗里有他的音乐，那听的人须要有恬静的思想同干净的耳朵。

冬夜——我们同外面的世界隔绝了——温文的莎士比亚不怎么拘礼地走进来了。这时，最好读《暴风雨》或者他自己的《冬夜故事》——

这两位诗人你不得不大声诵读——一个人独念，或者（有时凑巧）有一个人听着。一个以上——那就变做无聊的听众了。

趣味热烈紧张的书，很快地把我们带到说奇事的地方，这

---

6 Bishop Andrewes：十七世纪的英国神学家。

7 the gentle Shakespeare enters：即我们开始念莎翁作品的意思。

8 More than one—and it degenerates into an audience: If there is more than one listening to your reading, then it degenerates into an audience.

9 hurry on：传奇这类书，我们念的时节多半将那普通叙述的地方麻麻胡胡很快地看过，所注意的是那些惊心动魄的事情。

eye to glide over only. It will not do to read them out. I could never listen to even the better kind of modern novels without extreme irksomeness.

A newspaper, read out, is intolerable. In some of the Bank offices it is the custom (to save so much individual time) for one of the clerks —who is the best scholar[1]—to commence upon the *Times*, or the *Chronicle*, and recite its entire contents aloud pro bono publico[2]. With every advantage of lungs and elocution, the effect is singularly vapid. In barbers' shops and public-houses a fellow will get up, and spell out a paragraph, which he communicates as some discovery. Another fellow with his selection. So the entire journal transpires at length by piece-meal. Seldom-readers are slow readers, and, without this expedient, no one in the company would probably ever travel through[3] the contents of a whole paper.

Newspapers always excite curiosity. No one ever lays one down without a feeling of disappointment[4].

---

1 the best scholar：这自然是句讥笑话，不过指那在书记里比较懂得些事情的人，可是他在书记里却是"鹤立鸡群"。

2 pro bono publico: for the public benefit.

3 travel through: read over.

4 without a feeling of disappointment：Lamb是对现在没有热烈的趣味，而无时无刻不沉醉于过去的朦胧仙境的人，他最擅长的题材是"忆旧"。所以他对新闻纸没有什么爱好，他说过，"I cannot make these present

种书只好让眼睛溜掠看过去。把它读出声是不行的。我就是听人念那比较好些的近代小说，也免不了觉得万分的不耐烦。

一张报纸念出声来是使人忍耐不下的事。有些银行里有一种习惯，（为着省俭个人的时间，）让一个书记——他是里头最有学问的人——念出《泰晤士报》或者《纪事报》，大声地把"为公众的利益"的全部内容读出来。用尽肺同演说家的本领，那结果是非常无味的。在理发店同客栈里，一个人忽然站起来，拼着字念出一段新闻，他把这个告诉人家像个新发明。又一个拣他自己爱念的也报告一段出来。这样子整张报一块一块地最后全说出来了。少看书的人看字看得非常慢，若使没有这种变通办法，一群里恐怕没有一个人能够披阅完整张报纸的内容。

报纸总是引起我们的好奇心。可是没有一个人放下报纸时，心里不觉得失望。

---

times present to me." 深思好古的 Hawthorne 也说："I cannot understand the newspapers or history till it is at least a hundred years old." 凡是带这种癖性的人，写出的小品都情绪宛转缠绵，意味隽永，经得起我们的咀嚼，所以好的小品文家多半免不了钟情于已过去的陈迹或异代的轶闻，如 Montaigne 就是个显明的例子。

What an eternal time¹ that gentleman in black, at Nando's, keeps the paper! I am sick of hearing the waiter bawling out incessantly: "The *Chronicle* is in hand, sir."²

Coming in to an inn at night—having ordered your supper—what can be more delightful than to find lying in the window-seat, left there time out of mind by the carelessness of some former guest—two or three numbers of the old Town and Country Magazine, with its amusing tête-à-tête³ pictures—"The Royal Lover and Lady G—"; "The Melting Platonic⁴ and the Old Beau,"—and such-like antiquated scandal? Would you exchange it—at that time, and in that place—for a better book?

Poor Tobin who latterly fell blind, did not regret it so much for the weightier kinds of reading—*the Paradise Lost*, or *Comus*⁵, he could have read to him—but he missed the pleasure of skimming over with his own eye a magazine, or a light pamphlet.

I should not care to be caught in the serious avenues of some cathedral alone, and reading *Candide*⁶.

---

1 an eternal time：永久无终的时间（这是种常用的"艺增"说法）。

2 the waiter bawling out incessantly: "The *Chronicle* is in hand sir"：这是侍者答应向他要报来看的客人的话。

3 tête-à-têie: the being together of two persons alone.

4 Platonic：Plato 主张纯粹精神之爱，超乎肉体之爱情，所以精神的爱谓之 Platonic love，但俗人讥笑他这种学说，所以把它当作"唱高调"解了。

5 *The Paradise Lost* 和 *Comus* 俱是 Milton 的作品。

在那都俱乐部里，穿着黑衣的绅士拿那报纸看得多么久的年代了！侍者不断地叫着"先生，《纪事报》有人看着"，我真听得厌烦。

晚上到了个客栈——叫好了晚餐——在窗台上找出好久好久以前有些客人一时大意丢在那里——二三本小城的老杂志，带着两人对面的有趣图书——下面写着"伟大的爱人与格——太太"；"屈伏了的唱高调女人与老浪子"——同这一类久已过去了的谣言，天下还有比这个更快乐的事吗？你原〔愿〕意——在那时候，那样地方——把它来换一本更好的书吗？

最近瞎了眼睛的可怜杜宾对于不能阅览严重作品到〔倒〕没有什么痛惜——《失乐园》同《可吗斯》这类书他可以教人读给他听——但是他却失去了那用自己眼睛飞读杂志或者滑稽文章的快乐。

我就是在大教堂严肃的甬道里，独自读《戆第德》时候，若使给人看见，我也不怕什么。

---

6 *Candide*：法国服尔德（Voltaire）所作，有讥笑宗教的论调，因为 Voltaire 是个怀疑主义者。此书徐志摩先生有译本。

I do not remember a more whimsical surprise than having been once detected—by a familiar damsel—reclined at my ease upon the grass, on Primrose Hill (her Cythera[1]), reading—*Pamela*[2]. There was nothing in the book to make a man seriously ashamed at the exposure; but as she seated herself down by me, and seemed determined to read in company, I could have wished it had been—any other book. We read on very sociably for a few pages; and, not finding the author much to her taste, she got up, and—went away. Gentle casuist[3], I leave it to thee to conjecture, whether the blush (for there was one between us) was the property of the nymph or the swain[4] in this dilemma. From me you shall never get the secret.

I am not much a friend to out-of-doors reading. I cannot settle

---

1 Cythera：希腊神话中 Venus（青春的神）常到的山，Lamb 以这位小姐来比青春的神。

2 *Pamela*：十八世纪小说家 Richardson 著的小说，述一女仆名 Pamela，她的主人 Mr. B. 要她做外遇（Mistress），她坚执地拒绝，利诱威逼，终不能动。Mr. B. 佩服她的贞洁自爱，后来正式娶她。这部小说完全是她写给她父母的信，作文学史的人都认 Pamela 是英国真正小说的头胎娇儿。

3 casuist：一种于一切的行为专考究良心（动机）为何的人，议论精明，但太近于诡辩。De Quincey 有一篇有名的小品，论 casuistry。此处只作"研究人类行为的学者"解。

4 the nymph or the swain：水泽女神或牧羊少年。英国十七八世纪文人好以牧羊郎自况，来做情诗或他种诗歌，Milton 的 *Lycidas*（吊他大学朋友的哀歌）也是假设一个牧羊郎述他死后同伴哀悼的情形。Lamb 行文以十

我有一回很舒服地躺在草上，在樱草山（她的新使拿）被一个很熟的小姐侦出，在那里读——《拍买拉》，我记不起有过比这个更可笑的惊讶。书里并没有说什么话，使一个男人看起来，觉得真真地害羞；但是当她坐在我旁边，好像决心和我同念，我真望它是———本别的书。我们很要好地同念几页；她觉得这作家不合她的口胃，站起来——走了。温和的研究人们动机的学者，我让你去猜赧颜（我们中间有一个脸红了）在这两可的情形，倒〔到〕底是属于这位仙女，还是发生在我这田舍少年。你绝不能由我得到秘密。

我不大喜欢在户外读书。我不能够收下心读下去。我认得

七八世纪古文家为法，故用此种前朝滥调。但是 Lamb 摹仿十七八世纪的作家很能够得他们的神韵，却不至给他们束缚住了。他并且能运用古文，使生出好多诙谐来，所以他的文章比真正十七八世纪的散文大家的著作更饶兴趣。他那套古色斑烂〔斓〕的意思，好似一定要那种瑰奇巧妙的文体才能表现得出来，理想的文体是种由思想内心生出来的，结果和思想成一整个，互为表里，像灵魂同躯壳一样地不能离开——这种对于文体的学说是英国批评家自 Hazlitt 以至 Spencer, Pater, Middleton Murry 所公认的，也就是 Buffon 所谓 "The style is the man" 的意思。Lamb 文章所以那么引人入胜，也在于他思想和文体有不可分的关系。可见模仿古文，做古文都是无妨的，最要紧的是不能丢了自己的性格，而能运用奇怪的文体，将心灵更透彻地表现出，不然，又何贵乎模仿他人的调子，白使读者念时费力，又不能得到什么呢？

my spirits to it. I knew a Unitarian[1] minister who was generally to be seen upon Snow Hill (as yet Skinner's Street was not), between the hours of ten and eleven in the morning, studying a volume of Lardner[2]. I own this to have been a strain[3] of abstraction beyond my reach. I used to admire how he sidled along, keeping clear of secular contacts[4]. An illiterate encounter with a porter's knot[5], or a bread basket, would have quickly put to flight[6] all the theology I am master of[7], and have left me worse than indifferent to the five points.

There is a class of street-readers, whom I can never contemplate without affection—the poor gentry, who, not having wherewithal to buy or hire a book, filch a little learning at the open stalls—the owner, with his hard eye, casting envious looks at them all the while, and thinking when they will have done. Venturing tenderly, page after page, expecting every moment when he shall interpose his interdict, and yet unable to deny themselves the gratification, they "snatch a fearful joy." Martin B—, in this way, by daily fragments, got through[8] two volumes of *Clarissa*[9], when the stall-keeper damped his laudable ambition, by asking him (it was in his younger

---

1 Unitarian: 反对主张三位一体的教徒。
2 Lardner: 英国神道学家。
3 strain: severe demand upon faculties.
4 keeping clear of secular contacts: 这句有双关意，一是牧师独行慢读，和路人毫无接触；一是他驰心于神圣之言，忘却俗世的纷扰。

一个主张神位唯一派的牧师,他常常在早上十时同十一时中间,在雪山(师金吕街那时还没有出世)读一本腊得律做的书。这种忘却一切环境的能力,我自认是办不到的。看见一个挑夫的绳结或者一个面包篮会将我所知道的神学全由我脑里赶跑了,使我弄得比不知道五要点还坏。

还有一种路旁书摊的读者,我每次想起这种人我总要动情——那班可怜的先生,没有钱来买书同租书,由那排着书卖的摊子上偷些学问——老板,用他利害的眼睛,老在那里不高兴地看着,心里想什么时候他们才不看。悬心吊胆地冒险着,一页又一页,无时不在预期那老板会下个禁谕,但是他们又舍不得那种快乐,他们这样子"检〔捡〕来些充满恐惧的快乐"。马丁·伯——这样每天念一点,读完两卷克拉力沙,那时管摊子的冷下他这可赞美的野心,问他(这是在他年青时候)到底想不想

---

5 An illiterate encounter with a porter's knot: an encounter with an illiterate porter's knot. (Lamb 故意以 illiterate 形容 encounter,使文字意趣横生。)

6 put to flight: scare away.

7 am master of: know.

8 got through: read over.

9 *Clarissa*: Richardson 著的一篇很长的小说,共九大本。

days) whether he meant to purchase the work. M. declares, that under no circumstances of his life did he ever peruse a book with half the satisfaction which he took in those uneasy snatches. A quaint poetess[1] of our day has moralized upon this subject in two very touching but homely stanzas.

> I saw a boy with eager eye
> Open a book upon a stall,
> And read as he'd devour it all;
> Which when the stall-man did espy.
> Soon to the boy I heard him call,
> "You, Sir, you never buy a book,
> Therefore in one you shall not look."
> The boy pass'd slowly on, and with a sigh
> He wish'd he never had been taught to read,
> Then of the old churl's books he should have had no need.

> Of sufferings the poor have many,
> Which never can the rich annoy;
> I soon perceiv'd another boy,
> Who look'd as if he'd not had any

---

1 a quaint poetess：指 Lamb 的姊姊 Mary Lamb。

买那本书。老马说他一生中无论在什么情形之下，没有念一本书，有那次不安的偷看的一半趣味。一个现代奇怪的女诗人对这问题用两首非常动情，但是很朴素的诗来歌咏：

我看见一个眼睛充满热烈希望的小孩

在书摊上翻开一本书来，

读时节好似想一气念完；

开书摊人看见这样，

我听见他很快地向少年招呼。

"先生，你从来没有买过书，

所以请你不要在这里看书。"

小孩慢慢地踱开，叹口气，

满望他从来没有认过字母，

他就不会用这老东西的书了。

穷人有好多苦痛，

富的永远没有尝过；

我不久又看见一个小孩，

他脸上好像老是饿着，

Food, for that day at least—enjoy

The sight of cold meat in a tavern larder.

This boy's case, then thought I, is surely harder,

Thus hungry, longing, thus without a penny,

Beholding choice of dainty-dressed meat:

No wonder if he wish he ne'er had learn'd to eat.

那天最少是没吃东西——

他对着酒店的冻肉用着眼睛享受。

我想这个小孩的情形必定更苦,

这么饿着,想着,这样一个辨士也没有,

对着烹得精美的好肉空望:

他免不了会希望他生来没有学会吃东西。

(原载于1928年11月11日《文学周报》第7卷第18期,题名为《关于书籍与读书的杂感》,收入本集时改为此名)

William Hazlitt
(1778—1830)

On the Feeling of Immortality in Youth

No young man believes he shall ever die. It was a saying of my brother's, and a fine[1] one. There is a feeling of eternity in youth which makes us amends for everything[2]. To be young is to be as one of the immortals. One half of time indeed is spent—the other half remains in store[3] for us with all its countless treasures, for there is no line drawn[4], and we see no limit to our hopes and wishes. We make the coming age[5] our own—

"The vast, the unbounded prospect lies before us."

---

1 fine saying: good remark.
2 makes us amends for everything: gives us compensation for everything. (amends是复数。)
3 in store: laid up in readiness 预备好，等着用。
4 there is no line drawn: 就是没有限度的意思。

青年之不朽感

没有年青人相信他将来会死。这是我兄弟的话,真是一句妙语。年青人总觉他是能够长生不老,这情绪就可以赔偿我们一切的苦痛。青春时期的人可以说是个神仙。一半的光阴固然是用过去了——但是我们还有另一半预备着给我们用,包含了无穷的宝贝,因为我们不能够划清一条线,说下半生是那时截止,而且我们的希冀同愿望又是没有限度的。我们把将来都算做是我们的——

"我们前面浮现有浩大的无边的风光。"

---

5 the coming age: the future.

Death, old age, are words without a meaning, a dream, a fiction, with which we have nothing to do¹. Others may have undergone, or may still undergo them—we "bear a charmed life"², which laughs to scorn³ all such idle fancies. As, in setting out⁴ on a delightful journey, we strain our eager sight forward,

"Bidding the lovely scenes at distance hail,"

and see no end to prospect after prospect, new objects presenting themselves as we advance, so in the outset of life⁵ we see no end to our desires nor to the opportunities of gratifying them. We have as yet found no obstacle, no disposition to flag, and it seems that we can go on⁶ so for ever. We look round in a new world, full of life and motion, and ceaseless progress, and feel in ourselves all the vigour and spirit to keep pace⁷ with it, and do not foresee from any present signs how we shall be left behind in the race, decline into old age, and drop into the grave. It is the simplicity⁸ and, as it were, abstractedness⁹ of our feelings in youth that (so to speak) identifies us with

---

1 with which we have nothing to do: with which we are not concerned 那些和我们满不相干。
2 we "bear a charmed life": we are invulnerable 有魔力，他人不能损我们毫发。
3 laughs to scorn: treats as ridiculous 把……当做好笑的。
4 setting out: beginning journey.
5 the outset of life: the prime of life 年青时节。
6 go on: continue doing.

死同老变成没有意义的字,不过是梦幻的东西,和我们满不相干的。旁人挨过或者现在正受死老的苦——我们却"像有一种神秘的生命",敢对这些无聊的空想嘲笑。像一个快乐旅行开始时节,我们睁着热烈的眼睛前望,

"向远处的美景欢呼,"

我们走时,新东西接连地现在眼前,好景后面又有好景,简直没有尽处,同样地在我们生命起首期间,我们有不尽的愿望,我们以为满足愿望的机会也是无穷。我们还没有碰到障碍,不想歇步,仿佛我们可以永久这样前进。我们环视这充满生机进步不停的簇新世界,自己觉得也有精神力气可以跟它同走,我们现在看不出什么预征来推测将来我们会落后衰颓到变做老人,最终坠到墓里去。这是青春时我们知觉的感〔简〕单性,也可以说是抽象性(我们可以这样讲),使我们同自然合一,(因为

---

7 to keep pace: to go at equal speed.
8 simplicity:artlessness 头脑简单;老实坦白。
9 abstractedness:年青人多半偏于理想,对于一切事情缺乏具体的了解,所以说"年青人情感的抽象性"。

nature and (our experience being weak and our passions strong) makes us fancy ourselves immortal like it. Our short-lived¹ connection with being, we fondly² flatter ourselves, is an indissoluble and lasting union. As infants smile and sleep, we are rocked in the cradle of our desires³, and hushed into fancied security by the roar of the universe around us—we quaff the cup of life with eager thirst without draining it, and joy and hope seem ever mantling to the brim⁴—objects press around us, filling the mind with their magnitude and with the throng of desires that wait upon them, so that there is no room⁵ for the thoughts of death. We are too much dazzled by the gorgeousness and novelty of the bright waking dream⁶ about us to discern the dim shadow lingering for us in the distance. Nor would the hold⁷ that life has taken of us permit us to detach our thoughts that way, even if we could. We are too much absorbed in present objects and pursuits. While the spirit of youth remains unimpaired, ere "the wine of life is drunk,"⁸ we are like people intoxicated or in a fever, who are hurried

---

1 short-lived: brief.
2 fondly: foolishly.
3 the cradle of our desires: 年青人整天在希望里做梦，虽然世上波涛汹涌，也能够快乐地嬉笑过日，所以希望是我们的摇篮，使我们获得片刻的安眠。
4 mantling to the brim: foaming to the brim 杯缘满着白沫。
5 there is no room: there is no empty place.
6 the bright waking dream: "人生一梦"，所以世上一切都不过是一种

我们经验既少,情感又强)使我们想能够同自然一样长存不朽。我们痴痴地恭维自己以为我们这种和生命暂时的结合会永久不破。像小孩微笑着睡觉一样,我们在期望的摇篮中荡漾着,被环绕四旁的世界声音弄得静默地住在梦想的安全无忧境界里——我们焦渴地去饮生命之杯,并没有饮完,快乐同希望好像老满到杯缘地盛在杯中———切东西紧紧地围着我们,我们心中只去想这些东西的广大复杂同它们引起的欲望,所以我们没有空去想到死。我们这种醒时做的好梦太新鲜灿烂了,我们的眼睛太迷眩了,我们因此看不见那躲在远处等着我们的暗淡影子。就是说我们看见了,生命是这样紧地把我们擒住,它也不许我们分心那里去。我们真太给现在的物事吸引了。当青春的精神还完好无缺地存着,在"生命的酒饮干"以前,我们好似

醒时做的梦。

    7 the hold: the act of seizing or grasping in the hand 我们被"生命"迷惑着,等于在"生命"掌握之中。

    8 "the wine of life is drunk":把生命比做一杯酒,我们一天一天过去,好像是一口一口细尝着人生的滋味,及至真懂得人生味道的时候,杯已干了,死的时期也到来了。

away by the violence of their own sensations: it is only as present objects begin to pall upon the sense¹, as we have been disappointed in our favourite pursuits, cut off from our closest ties, that we by degrees become weaned² from the world, that passion loosens its hold upon futurity, and that we begin to contemplate as in a glass darkly the possibility of parting with it for good³. Till then, the example of others has no effect upon us. Casualties we avoid; the slow approaches of age we play at hide and seek with. Like the foolish fat scullion in Sterne⁴, who hears that Master Bobby is dead, our only reflection is, "So am not I!" The idea of death, instead of staggering our confidence, only seems to strengthen and enhance our sense of the possession and enjoyment of life. Others may fall around us like leaves, or be mowed down by the scythe of Time⁵ like grass: these are but metaphors to the unreflecting, buoyant cars and overweening presumption of youth. It is not till we see the flowers of Love, Hope and Joy withering around us, that we give up⁶ the flattering delusions that before led us on, and that the emptiness

---

1 to pall upon the sense: to dull the sense.
2 weaned：原来是"小孩断乳"的意思，这里作"对于世界无甚留恋"解。
3 for good：for ever, permanently 永远。
4 Sterne：十八世纪的英国的小说家，著有 *Tristram Shandy* 等书，以诙谐多感（sentimental）著名。
5 the scythe of Time：神话中"时间之神"拿着一把镰刀，表示许多东

喝醉了酒，或者有热病的人，给自己强烈的感情带着走：一定要等到对当前的事物，开始觉得乏味，爱干的事也灰心了，最密切的关系也割断了，我们才渐渐地忘却这世界，感情也没有那么猛烈地抓着将来，我们慢慢开始惨淡地想我们同世界永久分离的可能性，好像由一面镜子里看出。在那时期以前旁人的例子不能影响我们。不测的变故，我们避着不想；老年慢步的袭来，我们对他要捉迷藏。像斯天书里所说那个傻胖的厨子，听到他主人浦伯死的消息，他惟一的感想是"我却没有死！"我们通常也是这样。提起死这观念不仅不能把我们这自信摇动，倒反将我们现在享有生命的自觉增加力气。别人可以落叶般死在我们的四旁，蔓草也似地被"时间"的镰刀割下；这些话由那不加思索意气飞扬的耳朵同自负不凡妄加臆断的青春听来不过是几句漂亮的比喻就是了。非等到"爱情"，"希望"，"欣欢"的花一朵朵枯萎在我们四周，我们是不肯弃去以前引着我们向

西随时消灭，好像给镰刀刈去的一样。

  6 give up: part with or abandon 丢开。

and dreariness of the prospect before us reconciles us hypothetically to the silence of the grave.

Life is indeed a strange gift, and its privileges[1] are most mysterious. No wonder when it is first granted to us, that our gratitude, our admiration, and our delight should prevent us from reflecting on our own nothingness, or from thinking it will ever be recalled. Our first and strongest impressions[2] are borrowed from the mighty scene that is opened to us, and we unconsciously transfer its durability as well as its splendour to ourselves. So newly found, we cannot think of parting with it yet, or at least put off that consideration sine die[3]. Like a rustic at a fair, we are full of amazement and rapture, and have no thought of going home, or that it will soon be night. We know our existence only by ourselves, and confound our knowledge with the objects of it. We and Nature are therefore one. Otherwise the illusion, the "feast of reason and the flow[4] of soul, " to which we are invited, is a mockery and a cruel insult. We do not go from a play till the last act is ended, and the lights are about to be

---

1 privileges: 所谓生命的 "特权"，就是生命所给我们的各种趣味同快乐。

2 our first and strongest impressions: 指我们做小孩时最先得的印象（即青天大地以及自然景物）。

3 sine die (sī' nì dī' ē): indefinitely.

4 flow (*n.*): wine.

前走的幻影,到那时横在我们面前的空虚无趣的将来才使我们假说地不怕那坟墓里的寂静。

生命的确是一个奇怪的礼物,它的好处是非常神妙的。所以这事用不着纳罕,当这礼物初给我们时候,我们的感谢,赞美同快乐阻止我们记起我们本身的空虚渺茫,或者想到生命有一天会讨回去。我们生来第一次最深的印象是由对着我们开展的伟大自然得来的,我们不自觉地将自然的永存不灭性同壮丽辉煌处全移到自己身上。才得到世界,我们自然谈不到同它分手,最少也把这想头老是迟延着不提。好似在市场游玩的乡下人,我们心里充满了奇怪同高兴,并不想回家或者天快黑了这些事情。我们只能够根据自己去了解生命,我们又把智识同它的对象混在一起。因此我们同自然打成一片。若使不是这样子,那种幻觉,那种请我们去吃的"理智之宴同心灵之酒"全变做有意的讥笑同残酷的侮辱了。通常看戏要等最后一幕演完了,灯快灭了,我们才走出戏院。"自然"神仙般的庞儿老是美丽照

extinguished. But the fairy face of Nature still shines on; shall we be called away before the curtain falls, or ere we have scarce had a glimpse of what is going on¹? Like children, our step-mother Nature holds us up to see the raree-show² of the universe, and then, as if we were a burden to her to support, lets us fall down again. Yet what brave³ sublunary things does not this pageant present, like a ball or fête⁴ of the universe!

To see the golden sun, the azure sky, the outstretched ocean; to walk upon the green earth, and be lord of a thousand creatures; to look down yawning⁵ precipices or over distant sunny vales; to see the world spread out under one's feet on a map, to bring the stars⁶ near; to view the smallest insects through a microscope; to read history, and consider the revolutions of empire and the successions of generations; to hear of the glory of Tyre, of Sidon, of Babylon, and of Susa and to say all these were before me and are now nothing; to say I exist in such a point of time, and in such a point of space; to be a spectator and a part of its ever-moving scene; to witness the change of season, of spring and autumn, of winter and summer; to feel hot and cold, pleasure and pain, beauty and deformity, right and

---

1 what is going on: 戏台上所演的是什么。
2 raree-show（rār'ĭ-shō）: peep-show 西洋景。
3 brave: beautiful.

耀在宇宙的舞台上；在这出戏闭幕以前，或者当我们还看不清做的是什么时候，我们也得被召了去吗？像小孩子一样，我们被"自然"，我们的继母，捧起看一下西洋镜，不一会仿佛捧我们她也要费什么力气，又将我们放下了。可是，天下没有一件好东西不显在这镜里，像一个宇宙的跳舞或者大宴会。

看蔚蓝的苍天，金黄的太阳，舒卷的大海；走这碧绿的大地，做千种生物的主人；由张开大口的悬崖下望，或者远眺向阳的山谷；看世界像张地图展布在我们脚下；用天文仪把星拿近些来瞧；由显微镜看最小的昆虫；阅读历史，细想国家的革命同时代的递变；听到泰尔，锡顿，巴比伦，同苏沙的功绩，口里说这些全在我以前，现在却全化作乌有了；讲我是活在这一时期，这一地方；做这常动不停的世界舞台的观客，同时又扮一个角色；观察春夏秋冬四季的变换；尝到冷热苦乐美丑善恶

---

4 fête: festival or entertainment.
5 yawning:（壁立的岩石）好像"张开嘴打呵欠"的样子。
6 the stars：这指望远镜。

wrong; to be sensible to the accidents of nature; to consider the mighty world of eye and ear[1]; to listen to the stockdove's notes amid the forest deep; to journey over moor and mountain; to hear the midnight sainted choir[2]; to visit lighted halls, or the cathedral's gloom[3], or sit in crowded theatres and see life itself mocked[4]; to study the works of art and refine the sense of beauty to agony[5]; to worship fame, and to dream of immortality; to look upon the Vatican[6], and to read Shakespeare[7]; to gather up the wisdom of the ancients, and to pry into the future; to listen to the trump of war, the shout of victory; to question[8] history as to the movements of the human heart; to seek for truth; to plead the cause of humanity; to overlook the world as if time and nature poured their treasures at our feet—to be and to do all this, and then in a moment to be nothing—to have it all snatched from us as by a juggler's trick[9], or a phantasmagoria! There is something in this transition from all to nothing that shocks us and damps the entusiasm of youth new flushed with hope and pleasure, and we

---

1 the mighty world of eye and ear: 我们所看见的东西听见的声音。

2 the midnight sainted choir: 指圣诞之夜礼拜堂里的唱歌班。

3 the cathedral's gloom: 大礼拜堂进去很深, 光线多半不好, 所以有阴郁沉雄的气象。

4 see life itself mocked: 把真真的人生缩小起来放在舞台上, 岂不是同人生开玩笑? 此句或可解作"悲剧里面, 命运故意和人们捣乱, 冷酷地在旁嘲笑我们的孱弱无力"。

的不同；感觉到自然界的变更；细味那耳朵眼睛给我们的伟大世界；静听深林里斑鸠的歌调；旅游高山同泽地；午夜里默聆颂圣的乐声；到灯烛高照的大厅，或者赞美那壮大教堂的沉郁气象，或者坐在拥挤的戏院里看生命本身拿来嘲笑；研究艺术品，将审美能力磨练得使自己苦痛；崇拜名誉，梦想长生；瞻礼教皇的皇宫，诵读莎士比亚的戏剧；积起古人的智慧，再去探索将来；听战场的鼓角和凯旋的欢呼；根据着历史来考察人心的演化；找求真理；主张人道；俯视世界好像时间同自然倒出它们的宝贝在我们脚下——做这么复杂一个人，干这么多事，刹那间化作乌有——这么多的东西像幻影或者耍把戏的东西忽然由我们夺去！由这么复杂的境地一变变做什么都没有，这一转真够惊吓我们，沮丧那满涨了希望同快乐的少年热血，所以

---

5 to agony：to make desperate efforts 拚命。
6 Vatican：教皇住的地方。
7 Shakespeare：指莎士比亚的戏曲。
8 to question: to ask.
9 a juggler's trick：变戏法人能够将东西忽然变丢了。

cast the comfortless thought as far from as we can. In the first enjoyment of the state of life we discard[1] the fear of debts and duns, and never think of the final payment of our great debt to Nature[2]. Art we know is long; life, we flatter ourselves, should be so too. We see no end of the difficulties and delays we have to encounter; perfection is slow of attainment, and we must have time to accomplish it in. The fame of the great names we look up to is immortal: and shall not we who contemplate it imbibe a portion of ethereal fire, which nothing can extinguish? A wrinkle in Rembrandt[3] or in Nature takes whole days to resolve itself into its component parts, its softenings and its sharpnesses; we refine upon our perfections, and unfold the intricacies of nature. What a prospect for the future! What a task have we not begun! And shall we be arrested[4] in the middle of it? We do not count our time thus employed lost, or our pains thrown away; we do not flag or grow tired, but gain new vigour at our endless task. Shall Time, then, grudge[5] us to finish what we have begun, and have formed a compact with Nature to do? Why not fill up the blank that

---

1 discard: cast off.
2 the final payment of our great debt to Nature: 我们的身体本来是大自然给我们的，所以死去等于"将这笔债还给大自然"。
3 Rembrandt: 一个阴影画得工巧的画家。
4 arrested: stopt.
5 grudge: 舍不得。

我们远避这令人不安的思想。当开始享乐人生时候，我们丢开这欠债同迫偿的恐惧，就没有想起我们最后要还"自然"这笔大债。学是无涯，这我们晓得；我们恭维自己说生也是一样地无涯。我们知道要干一件事，我们遇着无限的困难同停顿；尽美尽善的地步是慢慢得到的，那么我们应当有时间去完成工作。我们所迎慕的大人物的盛名是不朽的；可是我们这班默想这盛名的人也能得些那什么也灭不了的灵气吗？屋能勃兰所画的或者"自然"所表现的一个皱纹，我们要花好几个整天才把它分析清楚，了解中间柔松尖硬的程度；我们陶炼那完好的东西，发阐出自然的奥妙。将来要干的事情有多少！我们已经动手做的工作是多么伟大！在事业没有成功以前，我们要被阻止吗？这样用去的时间，我们不把算做丢了，这样花的劳苦，我们不说是白费；我们没有灰心，也不厌倦，而且对这做不完的工作，我们的力气日日增加。这些我们已经动手，和"自然"也说好了，要干的事情，"时间"会鄙吝地不给我们光阴去弄完成吗？

is left us in his manner? I have looked for hours at a Rembrandt[1] without being conscious of the flight of time, but with ever new wonder and delight, have thought that not only my own but another existence I could pass in the same manner. This rarefied[2], refined existence seemed to have no end, nor stint[3], nor principle of decay in it. The print would remain long after I who looked on it had become the prey of worms. The thing seems in itself out of all reason: health, strength, appetite are opposed to the idea of death, and we are not ready to credit[4] it till we have found our illusions vanished, and our hopes grown cold. Objects in youth, from novelty, etc., are stamped upon the brain with such force and integrity[5] that one thinks nothing can remove or obliterate them. They are riveted there, and appear to us as an element of our nature. It must be a mere violence that destroys them, not a natural decay. In the very strength of this persuasion we seem to enjoy an age by anticipation. We melt down years into a single moment of intense sympathy, and by anticipating the fruits

---

1 a Rembrandt, 一张 Rembrandt 的画。Hazlitt 对图画嗜好甚深，关于该画写有几篇很好的小品，小品文家谈画的除了 Hazlitt 之外，要算那位爱狗的医生 Horal Subsecival 和《闲时》的作者 Dr. John Brown 以及现代著名的小品文家 E. V. Lucas 了。
2 rarefied: spiritual 精神方面的。
3 stint: limitation.
4 credit: believe.
5 integrity: entirety.

这功败于垂成之际以后的时间,为什么不送给我们呢?我曾经连着几个钟头细看一张屋能勃兰的图画,不觉时间的飞过,只是每回都带着新的奇怪同快乐想,不仅我这一生,就是再有一生也可以这样地过去。这种高雅微妙的生活似乎是不会有终止的,没有限定日期,也并不包含有衰颓的分子。我这个看画的人化做蠕虫的食料后,这画还可以留存好久。死这回事像个完全不合理的,我们平常的健康,力气,嗜欲没有一个情形对这死的观念不是相反的,一定要等到我们的幻觉毁灭,我们的希望冰冷,我们才预备去相信天下有死这一回事。年青时节一切东西因为新鲜同别的原因特别有力整个地印在脑上,我们以为没有东西可以抹去或者破坏这些印象。这些印象钉在脑中,由我们看来是我们的一部分了。我们相信要去丢这些印象必定用暴力,天然的朽腐是不行的。我们这种信力坚固时,我们好像将长生的快乐在意想中提前享来。所以靠着强烈的领悟,我们镕化几十载做了一刻,用了这关于未来的推测,我们来抵抗时

defy the ravages of time. If, then, a single moment of our lives in worth years, shall we set any limits to its total value and extent? Again, does it not happen that so secure do we think ourselves of an indefinite period of existence, that at times, when left to ourselves[1], and impatient of novelty, we feel annoyed at what seems to us the slow and creeping progress of time, and argue that if it always moves at this tedious snail's pace it will never come to an end? How ready are we to sacrifice any space of time which separates us from a favourite object, little thinking that before long[2] we shall find it move too fast.

For my part, I started in life with the French Revolution, and I have lived, alas! to see the end of it.[3] But I did not foresee this result. My sun arose with the first dawn of liberty[4], and I did not think how soon both must set. The new impulse to ardour given to men's minds

---

1 left to ourselves: alone.
2 before long: soon.
3 For my part, ... the end of it: 当法国革命开始时，英国文人如 Wordsworth, Coleridge, Southey, Hazlitt 等，对它表示热烈的同情，Wordsworth 甚至亲身跑到法国，幸亏他的亲友设法把他找回来，不然他也上了断头台了。以后法国革命弄得一塌糊涂，民众只知乱杀，拿破仑窃取政权，做起皇帝来，于是从前抱着满怀希望的文士一个个心情都冰冷下去，反变做守旧派了。Wordsworth 灰心事业，跑到山里做他的田园诗，Hazlitt 也壮志顿消，失意地骂骂些人。后来 Browning 提到这回事，

间的蹂躏。那么若使我们生命里一刻就值得几十载,我们对生命全体的价值同长短还要加什么限度吗?我们不是有时对自己的生命没有终点这样事很有把握,当一个人独在一块心里不耐烦想翻些新花样时候,我们对这由我们看来同爬着一样慢的时间步伐真觉厌倦,私下打算倘然时间老是这般蜗牛似地无聊地移动,这时间简直过不完?我们心爱东西还没到手时节,我们多么愿意牺牲这中间的时光,一点也没有想到不久我们会感到时间走得太快了。

至于我自己,我生在法国革命时期,我活到,唉呵!看见它的终局。可是我并没有预料到这结果。我的生命跟这自由的曙光同来,我从前没有想到多么快这两件东西都要沉灭。这给人们以热狂的新刺激,也给我心一种同样的热情;那时我们都

说 Wordsworth 忽然换个色彩,这种矛盾行为是不对,还做了一首 *Our Lost Leader* 的诗来讥讽他,那未免有些冤枉这位老诗人了。

4 the first dawn of liberty:指一七八九年法国革命的起事——攻破 Bastille 狱。

imparted a congenial[1] warmth and glow to mine; we were strong to run a race together, and I little dreamed that long before mine was set, the sun of liberty would turn to blood, or set once more in the night of despotism[2]. Since then, I confess, I have no longer felt myself young, for with that my hopes fell.

I have since turned my thoughts to gathering up some of the fragments of my early recollections, and putting them into a form to which I might occasionally revert. The future was barred to my progress, and I turned for consolation and encouragement to the past[3]. It is thus that, while we find our personal and substantial identity vanishing from us, we strive to gain a reflected and vicarious one[4] in our thoughts: we do not like to perish wholly, and wish to bequeath our names, at least, to posterity. As long as we can make our cherished thoughts and nearest interests[5] live in the minds of others, we do not appear to have retired altogether from the stage[6]. We still

---

1 congenial: of kindred temper with others 法国的革命精神鼓舞起年青的 Hazlitt 的热血。

2 the sun of liberty would turn to blood, or set once more in the night of despotism: 指暴民专制的残杀和暴王专制的黑暗。

3 I turned for consolation and encouragement to the past: Hazlitt 对于"过去"看得比"现在"还重,他是一个恋着肉化血枯的骸骨的人,曾做过一篇绝妙的小品文,论"过去与将来"。本来回忆是小品文作家的一种好法子,不管什么东西,经过时间宝库的贮藏,拿出来都觉得带有缥缈

意气雄壮，大可以同跑一趟光荣的路，我万想不到在我的生命还没有尽以前，自由的朝阳居然早已化做赤血或者又落到专制的黑夜里。我自认从那时候起我就不再觉得自己是个青年，因为我的希望跟着也倒下了。

以后我转过心来，把早年事的回忆想零零碎碎地收集起来，写下备我自己有时翻看。我向将来的前进被截止了，我只好向过去找些安慰同鼓舞。所以当我们发觉自己实实在在的生命渐渐离开了我们消灭，我们就努力在思想里去得一个反映的，可以拿来做代表的生命；我们不愿全部沦亡，希望最少我们的名可以传到后世。当我们能够使旁人心里想到我们心爱的思想同切己的事情时候，我们并不像完全退出这舞台。我们在旁人心

蕴藉的气概，格外有趣，那种妙处正如白云罩着半露天外的远山一样。Charles Lamb最善于做这种文章。

4 a reflected and vicarious one：我们的过去同我们的思想都是我们全人格的一部分；把这些写下，也可以做我们的代表。

5 nearest interests: interests nearest to our heart.

6 stage：世界一戏场，莎士比亚也说过"The world is but a stage"。

occupy the breasts of others, and exert an influence and power over them, and it is only our bodies that are reduced to dust and powder. Our favourite speculations still find encouragement, and we make as great a figure in the eye of the world, or perhaps a greater, than in our lifetime. The demands of our self-love are thus satisfied, and these are the most imperious and unremitting. Besides, if by our intellectual superiority we survive ourselves in this world, by our virtues and faith we may attain an interest in another, and a higher state of being, and may thus be recipients at the same time of men and of angels[1].

"E'en from the tomb the voice of Nature cries,

E'en in our ashes live their wonted fires."

As we grow old, our sense of the value of time becomes vivid. Nothing else, indeed, seems of any consequence. We can never cease wondering that that[2] which has ever been should cease to be. We find many things remain the same; why then should there be change in us. This adds a convulsive grasp of whatever is[3], a sense of a fallacious hollowness in all we see. Instead of the full, pulpy[4] feeling of youth tasting existence and every object in it[5], all is flat

---

1 recipients at the same time of men and of angels: 人虽然厕身在神仙之列，心却仍留连于人间的祸福。

2 前一个that是conjunction；后一个that是pronoun，当做subject用。

3 whatever is: 无论什么存在的东西。(is: exists.)

4 pulpy: juicy.

中还占有地位，对他们生出影响，化作尘埃的只是我们的身体；我们喜欢的思想还是受人欢迎，在世人眼中我们有同样的地位，或者比生时更要出色。这样子，就可以满足我们自爱的要求，一个紧迫毫不放松的要求。而且若使我们知识的优长能够使我们肉体死了，精神不死，那么用我们的道德信仰，我们亦可达到对别人发生趣味，自己生活也可以有更高尚的境界，这样子我们同时能做天使同人们的伴侣。

"自然之声是从坟墓之中出来；

他们昔日之火焰仍存在我们的灰烬之中。"

我们年纪一大，我们明显地感觉到时间的宝贵，真的，别的东西全没有什么重要。我们老是奇怪，已经有过的为什么会变做没有。我们知道许多东西总是一样地丝毫不差；那为什么我们会变老呢。这念头叫我们加紧地抓着现在，使我们深感到我们看见的一切是空虚幻假。失丢了在初尝生活同一切东西时候那

---

5 existence and every object in it：世界及世界里面一切东西。

and vapid, —a whited sepulchre, fair without but full of ravening and all uncleanness within. The world is a witch that puts us off[1] with false shows and appearances. The simplicity of youth, the confiding expectation, the boundless raptures, are gone: we only think of getting out of it as well as we can, and without any great mischance or annoyance[2]. The flush of illusion, even the complacent retrospect of past joys and hopes[3], is over; if we can slip out of life without indignity, can escape with little bodily infirmity, and frame[4] our minds to the calm and respectable composure of still-life before we return to physical nothingness[5], it is as much as we can expect. We do not die wholly at our deaths; we have mouldered away gradully long before. Faculty after faculty, interest after interest, attachment after attachment disppear; we are torn from ourselves[6] while living, year after year sees us no longer the same, and death only consigns the last fragment of what we were[7] to the grave.

---

1 put us off: waste our time.

2 and without any great mischance or annoyance: 这篇文章由少年英气勃勃的情怀说到老年万念俱灰的心境，那种对人生的疲倦，真是人生的缩影，和 Andreyev 剧曲《人的一生》可以比较一下。

3 the complacent retrospect of past joys and hopes: 不止对现在不感到趣味，对将来不存些希望，就是火炉之旁，树荫之下的静默的回忆，也不能使这麻木的心灵有些须的高兴：到这种地步，真可说这你来我去的世界是毫无足留恋了。

种丰满流畅的少年精神，什么都是平凡无味——世界变做一个粉饰的坟墓，外面是漂亮的，里头充满了蠕虫争食同一切的不洁。世界是一个女巫，拿假玩意儿来骗骗人。但是青年的老实，不疑的期望，无涯的欣欢全消散了：我们只打算怎样好好地走出世界，没有碰什么大麻烦或者大祸患。幻觉的灿烂丢了，就是那怡然自乐，对过去的快乐同已灭的希望的回忆也找不到；若使我们办到能够没有受侮辱地走出生命行列，身体也无大损伤地逃出，在归到大虚以前心境可以修养得同槁木死灰一样地恬静安宁，——这就是我们最大的希望。我们不在死时完全死；老早我们已经渐渐地腐朽了。机官随着机官，趣味跟着趣味，一个个癖好继续掉去；我们活时节，生就已由我们身上剥去，岁岁年年人不同，死不过是将从前的我们的最后剩下的残碎搁在墓里。

---

4 frame: adapt.
5 physical nothingness：指死后的肉腐骨化。
6 torn from ourselves："渐渐地，一部部死去"的意思。
7 what we were：从前的我们。

That we should wear out¹ by slow stages, and dwindle at last into nothing, is not wonderful, when even in our prime our strongest impressions leave little trace but for the moment² , and we are the creatures of petty circumstance. How little effect is made on us in our best days³ by the books we have read, the scenes we have witnessed, the sensations we have gone through! Think only of the feelings we experience in reading a fine romance (one of Sir Walter's⁴, for instance); what beauty, what sublimity, what interest, what heart-rending emotions! You would suppose the feelings you then experienced would last⁵ for ever, or subdue⁶ the mind to their own harmony and tone: while we are reading it seems as if noting could ever put us out of our way⁷, or trouble us: —the first splash of mud that we get on entering the street, the first twopence we are cheated out of, the feeling vanishes clean out of our minds, and we become the prey of petty and annoying circumstance⁸. The mind soars to the lofty⁹: it is at home¹⁰ in the grovelling, the disagreeable,

---

    1 wear out: gradually consume and waste by use.
    2 for the moment: not lasting a long time.
    3 our best days: our young days.
    4 Sir Walter Scott：十九世纪浪漫派的小说大家，以写历史小说——偏于苏格兰及中古时代的名于世，著作甚多。
    5 last: remain alive.
    6 subdue: assimilate.

我们这样次第销磨下去，一直销到没有，用不着什么惊愕，因为在我们年富力强时期，我们最深的印象也不过暂时留在脑中，我们本是受细微环境支配的动物。我们一生中最好的时期中，所读的书，看的事情，受的刺激对我们生下的影响是多么少呀！试想读本好传奇（比方说，司各德的）时候，我们当时感情的经验如何；多么壮丽，多么有趣，多么使人心碎！你一定猜这些情调可以常留不灭，或者将你的心化做同样气质腔调；我们念时节，好像天下没有什么事情能够搅乱我们这心境，或者使我们感到麻烦：——但是一走到街第，脚上沾污了的第一块泞泥，被人骗去的第一个两辨士就够使我们的情调由心中完全隐没去，我们变做微末，麻烦的环境的战利品了。我们的心虽然向高尚卓越处飞翔，它却总是和卑污的，可厌的以及微小的事

---

    7 put us out of our way: stagger our present mental state.
    8 the prey of petty and annoying circumstance：读者千万不要误会 Hazlitt 是主张唯物史观的，他在另一篇小品《思想与行为》上曾主张意志万能的学说。
    9 the lofty: the ideal realm.
    10 is at home: is perfectly familiar with.

and the little. And yet we wonder that age[1] should be feeble and querulous, —that the freshness of youth should fade away. Both worlds[2] would hardly satisfy the extravagance of our desires and of our presumption.

---

1 age: old man.
2 both worlds: this world and next world.

情熟识。然而我们还是奇怪老人身体会衰弱,爱发牢骚——少年人的青春会萎谢凋零。实在说起来,天上同人间这两世界合起来,也不容易满足我们过度的希望同骄傲。

Leigh Hunt

(1784—1859)

Watchmen

The readers of these our fourpenny lucubrations[1] need not be informed that we keep no carriage. The consequence is, that being visitors of the theatre, and having some inconsiderate friends who grow pleasanter and pleasanter till one in the morning, we are great walkers home by night; and this has made us great acquaintances[2] of watchmen, moonlight, mud-light[3], and other accompaniments of that interesting hour[4]. Luckily we are fond of[5] a walk by night. It does not always do us good; but that is not the fault of the hour, but our

---

1 lucubrations: compositions of a learned or too elaborate and pedantic character 繁征博引的论文。Leigh Hunt 这篇文章载在他所办的小报叫做 Companion 上面，Companion 所登的都是轻快有趣的文字。Leigh Hunt 故意说是 lucubrations，是一种说反话的滑稽。

2 great acquaintances: 对那些人物景色很熟识，仿佛是位老朋友。

更　　夫

　　看我们这四辨士一份的议论的读者，用不着通知，自然晓得我们是没有家车的。我们爱看戏，又有几个不小心的朋友时间越迟，越玩得高兴一直到晚上一点钟才止，结果我们变做深夜回家的步行大家，所以我们和更夫，月夜，泥土的光，同这有趣时候别的东西都非常熟识。很侥幸，我们本来爱夜里步行。这样事不一定对身体有益；但是这并不是时间太迟的罪过，是

　　3　mud-light：moonlight 洁明可爱，mud-light 自然没有什么好处，一个普照天上，一个在沟里发光，Leigh Hunt 却故意选同是 m 开头的字，以字面的相似，更衬出二个的不同了。
　　4　interesting hour：指夜深时。
　　5　are fond of: like.

own, who ought to be stouter; and therefore we extract what good we can out of our necessity, with becoming¹ temper. It is a remarkable thing in nature, and one of the good-naturedest things² we know of her³, that the mere fact of looking about us, and being conscious of what is going on⁴, is its own reward, if we do but notice it in good-humour⁵. Nature is a great painter (and art and society are among her works), to whose minutest touches the mere fact of becoming alive⁶ is to enrich the stock of our enjoyment⁷.

We confess there are points liable to cavil⁸ in a walk home by night in February. Old umbrellas have their weak sides; and the quantity of mud and rain may surmount the picturesque. Mistaking a soft piece of mud for hard, and so filling your shoe with it, especially at setting out, must be acknowledged to be "aggravating"⁹. But then you ought to have boots. There are sights, indeed, in the streets

---

1 becoming: proper; good.

2 one of the good-naturedest things: 前面有 nature 一字，这里又用 good-naturedest，重复得非常巧妙有趣。

3 her: nature是阴性，我们常说Mother Nature，因为自然给我们一切，简直像个抚育小孩的慈母。

4 what is going on: what appears before us 本来说到做戏时，going on 才作这样解 (to appear on the stage)，这处是借用，把世界比做一个大舞台。

5 good-humour: 这句可表现出 Leigh Hunt 对人生的态度。他一生痛快淋漓，无往而不自得，有一回他做文章不小心，骂皇太子几句，给地方官抓去关在狱中，他却将囚室墙上挂了许多图画，还排了好几架书，室外小地又遍栽花木，爱说笑话的 Lamb 跑去狱中望他，看见他这种安乐神气，

我们的错处，我们应当生得强壮些；因此我们要客客气气地由这不得已的情形中找出我们所能得的好处。这是"大自然"奇怪的一点，我们所知道她最和蔼可亲的一个地方，当你向四面一望，又明白了那时的情境，若使你心里是快活，这一看就可报偿给你许多趣味。"大自然"是一个大画家（艺术同社会也是她的作品），若使对她极细微的一笔能够鉴赏感动，我们快乐的材料就丰富得多了。

我们也承认在二月晚上步行回家有好多地方会被人指摘，说有毛病。旧伞有它的坏处；泥土同大雨的量可以超过好景致。一个软的泥块错当做硬的，弄得满鞋是土，特别在出发时候，无论如何，要算做使人难堪。然而你应当穿长靴。的确伦敦街

冲口说道，若使世上有天堂，那一定就是这里了。

6 alive: sensible.

7 the stock of our enjoyment：许多小品文作家的目的，不过是把我们的趣味增加，所以对于世上各种物事，常用一种特别眼光来看，为的是这样可以将我们趣味的范围扩张，并不一定有什么"立异为高，逆情于誉"。

8 liable to cavil: open to cavil，容易受人指摘。

9 aggravating: annoying; irritating.

of London, which can be rendered pleasant by no philosophy[1]; things too grave to be talked about in our present paper; but we must premise, that our walk leads us out of town, and though streets and suburbs of by no means[2] the worst description. Even there we may be grieved if we will. The farther the walk into the country, the more tiresome we may choose to find it; and when we take it purely to oblige others, we must allow, as in the case of a friend of ours, that generosity itself on two sick legs[3] may find limits to the notion of virtue being its own reward[4], and reasonably "curse those comfortable people" who, by the lights in their windows, are getting into their warm beds, and saying to one another—"Bad thing to be out of doors to-night."

Supposing then that we are in a reasonable state of health and comfort in other respects, we say that a walk home at night has its merits, if you choose to meet with them[5]. The worst part of it is the setting out, —the closing of the door upon the kind faces that part with you. But their words and looks on the other hand may set you well off[6]. We have known a word last us all the way home, and a

---

    1 philosophy: superiority to pain and passions, 达观。
    2 by no means: certainly not.
    3 generosity itself on two sick legs: 就是"慷慨"的化身，两脚酸痛地，却要陪人走路，恐怕也会不高兴罢。
    4 virtue being its own reward: 这是一句熟语，勉励人修德。

上有些事情，无论什么哲学也不能把它变做可爱；那类事情说起来太严重了，不合在我们这纸上讨论；可是我们要声明，我们走的路程带我们离开城市，我们所走的街道同近郊绝不是那最糟的。然而就在我们走的地方，若使我们要伤心，也有伤心的可能。我们走到乡下走得愈远，我们会觉得愈疲倦；若使我们完全是陪朋友走，我们不能不承认，（我们的一位朋友就在这样情形过，）两只酸痛脚上的慷慨会使人感到为善本身就是快乐这句话用的地方不能普遍，同时我们可以很有理由地"诅那班舒服的人们"，他们窗上的灯光照出他们正到暖和的床铺去，互相说道——"今晚在外面走的人真苦呀。"

假设我们的健康同别的安适的准备都还可以，我们可以说，你若想去找些好处，夜行回家也有它的好处。最苦的部分是在出发时候，——大门把同你分别的慈爱脸孔遮住时候。但是他们的话同面容有时却可以带你好好地走一大阵的路。我们经验

---

5 choose to meet with them: determine to them in good spirit.
6 set you well off: begin your journey happily.

look make a dream of it. To a lover, for instance, no walk can be bad. He sees but one face[1] in the rain and darkness; the same that he saw by the light in the warm room. This ever accompanies him, looking in his eyes; and if the most pitiable and spoilt face in the world should come between them, startling him with the saddest mockery of love, he would treat it kindly for her sake. But this is a begging of the question[2]. A lover does not walk. He is sensible neither to the pleasures nor pains of walking. He treads on air; and in the thick[3] of all that seems inclement, has an avenue of light and velvet spread for him, like a sovereign prince.

To resume then, like men of this world[4]. The advantage of a late hour is, that everything is silent, and the people fast in their beds. This gives the whole world a tranquil appearance. Inanimate objects are no calmer than passions and cares now seem to be, all laid asleep. The human being is motionless as the house or the tree; sorrow is suspended; and you endeavour to think, that love only is awake. Let not readers of true delicacy be alarmed, for we mean to

---

1 one face: i.e. his lover's face.
2 begging of the question: assuming the thing to be proved，以不确实的事情做前提，来推论下去。
3 in the thick: at the most crowded.
4 men of this world: 凡人。

过一句话够我们想了整个归程，一个面容使我们做梦地走到家里。譬如由一个正在恋爱热狂中的人看来，没有道路是坏的。在大雨昏黑里面，他只看见一个脸孔，就是在暖和房子灯光底下所看的脸孔。这总是跟他走，在他眼睛的前面；设使世界上顶可怜的憔悴脸孔忽然现在当前，用这对爱情最可悲的嘲笑来吓他，他为她的缘故也会仁爱地看待。但是这一大阵话是用靠不住的事拿来当大前提。一个爱人压根儿就不走路。他既尝不出走路的快乐，也不知道什么苦痛。他踏着云走，在好像严酷苦痛的环境里头，他有一条光明的路，铺着天鹅绒让他皇帝一样地走过。

回过来，让我们像普通的人谈一谈夜行罢。深夜的好处在于什么东西都寂默着，人们熟睡在床上。全世界因此有一种恬静的气象。情感同思虑现在全睡得同死的东西一样地安定。人们像房屋同树林不动地躺着；悲哀是停止了；你心里打算只有爱情才清醒罢。请神经灵敏的读者不要害怕，我们对应当奉为

touch profanely upon nothing that ought to be sacred; and as we are for thinking the best on these occasions, it is of the best love we think; love, of no heartless order, legal or illegal[1]; and such only as ought to be awake with the stars.

As to cares, and curtain-lectures[2], and such-like abuses of the tranquillity of night, we call to mind, for their sakes, all the sayings of the poets and others, about "balmy sleep", and the soothing of hurt minds, and the weariness of sorrow, which drops into forgetfulness. The great majority are certainly "fast as a church" by the time we speak of; and for the rest, we are among the workers who have been sleepless for their advantage[3]; so we take out our licence to forget them for the time being. The only thing that shall remind us of them, is the red lamp, shining afar over the apothecary's door; which, while it does so, reminds us also that there is help for them to be had. I see him now, the pale blinker, suppressing the conscious injustice of his anger[4] at being roused by the apprentice, and fumbling himself out of the house, in hoarseness and great coat, resolved to

---

 1 love, of no heartless order, legal or illegal：不论是经过法律手续或者没有经过法律手续也好，只要是真心相爱就是神圣的婚姻了。
 2 curtain-lectures：女人晚上教训她丈夫的话。
 3 who have been sleepless for their advantage：Leigh Hunt 晚上出去闲逛，观察夜间景色，描写来供读者鉴赏，所以他可算是一个晚间工作的人了。

神圣的东西不想侮慢；我们在这时候所想的既然全是最好的，我们所说的爱情也是最纯洁的；不是那种合法或者不合法的没有真心的爱情；只是那配得上跟星光同时醒着的。

至于那些焦虑呀，帐中说法呀，同这类伤害夜里安宁的事情，想到它们，我们特地记起诗人等等说的嘉言，什么"甜香的安眠"呀，创伤的心的慰抚，同悲哀的疲倦送人到忘却一切的境地这类话。大多数人在我们说的这个时候一定是教堂似地安息；其余呢，我们也是为这大多数的利益没有去睡的工作者；因此我们有特权可以暂时忘记他们。惟一引起我们留意到他们的东西是那红灯，远远地照在药铺门口的上头；这灯发光时候，使我记起这大多数若使要得救助，可以来这儿找。我现在看见那医生脸色苍白，眯着眼睛，压下那对把他叫醒的学徒的不合理的生气，麻麻糊糊走出房子，声音粗哑，穿件大氅，私下打

---

4 the conscious injustice of his anger：医生被徒弟叫醒，心里一团不高兴，想向徒弟发脾气，但自己知道这不是徒弟的错，所以只好吞下气了。

make the sweetness of the Christmas bill¹ indemnify him for the bitterness of the moment.

But we shall be getting too much into the interior of the houses. By this time the hackney-coaches have left all the stands²; a good symptom of their having got their day's money. Crickets are heard, here and there, amidst the embers of some kitchens. A dog follows us. Will nothing make him "go along"³? We dodge him in vain; we run; we stand and "hish" at him; accompanying the prohibition with dehortatory gestures, and an imaginary picking up of a stone. We turn again, and there he is, vexing our skirts. He even forces us into an angry doubt whether he will not starve, if we do not let him go home with us. Now if we could but lame him without being cruel; or if we were only an overseer⁴; or a beadle⁵; or a dealer in dog-skin; or a political economist⁶, to think dogs unnecessary. Oh, come; he has turned a corner; he is gone; we think we see him trotting off at a distance, thin and muddy; and our heart misgives us. But it was not our fault; we were not "hishing" at the time. His

---

1 the Christmas bill: 英俗各店铺在圣诞节收帐，所以他们的圣诞节等于我们的除夕。
2 stands: chosen standing-ground.
3 go along: get you gone.
4 overseer: 区里管事人，可以发命令捕杀狗。
5 beadle: 同overseer有同样的权力。

定主意用圣诞节开帐要钱时数单的甜蜜来报偿他这刻的辛苦。

这么说下去,我们要说太多房子里面的事情了。这时候野鸡马车全离开它们常站的地方;他们今天挣到钱的一个好现象。几个厨房的燃屑中,到处可以听到蟋蟀叫。一条狗跟我们走。没有法子可以使他"滚开"吗?我们躲避他,白费了力气;我们跑着;站住对他"嘘";禁止时还带了劝戒的姿势同假假地检〔捡〕块石头。我们拐一湾〔弯〕,他还在那里缠绕我们的衣裳。他简直逼得我们愤怒地怀疑我们不让他随我们到家,他会不会挨饿。若使我们能够弄跛他而不带一丝残忍,若使我们是地方管事人,吏役或者卖狗皮的人,或者一个想狗是不必需的经济学者,那是多么好呀!啊,好;在基角上他拐湾〔弯〕了;走去了;我们觉得看得见他身体消瘦踉跄在远处飞跑;我们的心中却难过得很。但是这不是我们的错;他走时候我们并没有"嘘"他。他这样

---

6 political economist:这是讥笑那班经济家无论对什么事情,只看有用没有用,全不想到别的方面。经济学家所以叫做 political economist,因为从前 Aristotle 分经济为三种,即皇家经济,私人经济同国家经济,现在普通所谓经济是属于这第三种。

departure was lucky, for he had got our enjoyments into a dilemma; our "article" would not have known what to do with him. These are the perplexities to which your sympathizers are liable[1]. We resume our way, independent and alone; for we have no companion this time, except our never-to-be-forgotten and ethereal companion, the reader. A real arm within another's puts us out of the pale of walking that is to be made good[2]. It is good already. A fellow pedestrian is company; is the party you have left; you talk and laugh, and there is no longer anything to be contended with[3]. But alone, and in bad weather, and with a long way to go, here is something for the temper and spirits to grapple with and turn to account[4]; and accordingly we are booted and buttoned up, an umbrella over our heads, the rain pelting upon it, and the lamp-light shining in the gutters; "mudshine," as an artist of our acquaintance used to call it, with a gusto of reprobation. Now, walk cannot well be worse; and yet it shall be nothing[5] if you meet it heartily. There is a pleasure in overcoming any obstacle; mere action is something; imagination is more; and the spinning of the blood,

---

1 your sympathizers are liable: 一面怕狗难过,一面又要顾到自己,所以富于同情心的人常有这种进退两难的时候。

2 to be made good: in need of a good spirit to make it happy.

3 to be contended with: to be struggled against.

4 turn to account: make serviceable.

5 it shall be nothing: it shall not be a burden.

离开去是很侥幸的,他把我们快乐变做狼狈两难情形;我们这篇"文章"会不知道怎地处置他好。这些困难情形,有同情心的人都很容易遇到。现在我们再走我们的路,独自孤单地;因为这时除开我们从来不会忘记的渺茫朋友,我们的读者外,我们没有别的伴侣。把个真的手臂插在别人手臂里,已经不是要想法子才能快活的步行了。因为那已经是很好了。一个步行的同志就可算伴侣了,可以等于你才离开的那群朋友;一路有说有笑,用不着什么奋斗了。但是孤单单地凄风冷雨里要走一程长路,这才用得到毅力同耐性支持着;于是我们穿上长靴,紧紧扣起衣衫,撑着伞,雨滴打到伞上,灯光照小沟发亮;还有"泥块的光",一个艺术家,我们的朋友,常常一团不高兴地说这两字。现在,步行不能找一个再坏的环境了;但是若使你高兴地干去,这些麻烦都不值什么。打倒个障碍本来是个快事;仅仅动作已经可得快乐;想像更添上许多趣味;血脉的加快流

and vivacity of the mental endeavour, act well upon one another, and gradually put you in a state of robust consciousness[1] and triumph. Every time you set down your leg, you have a respect for it. The umbrella is held in the hand, like a roaring trophy.

We are now reaching the country: the fog and rain are over; and we meet our old friends the watchmen, staid, heavy, indifferent, more coat than man, pondering yet not pondering[2], old but not reverend, immensely useless. No, useless they are not; for the inmates of the houses think them otherwise, and in that imagination they do good. We do not pity the watchmen as we used[3]. Old age often cares little for regular sleep. They could not be sleeping perhaps, if they were in their beds; and certainly they would not be earning. What sleep they get, is perhaps sweeter in the watchbox, —a forbidden sweet[4]; and they have a sense of importance, and a claim on the persons indoors, which together with the amplitude of their coating and the possession of the box itself, make them feel themselves, not without reason, to be "somebody"[5]. They are peculiar and official. Tomkins

---

1 robust consciousness: the consciousness of strength.

2 pondering yet not pondering：看更夫年迈龙钟，沉默严肃的样子，好像是在那里想什么事，但是这班糊涂的老头子莫名其妙地度日，实在什么也不想。

3 used: used to pity them 往常那样子可怜他们。

4 a forbidden sweet：更夫晚上应当清醒，在更棚里偷睡，自然是一种违法的痛快事情。

转同精神的努力活泼互相影响，渐渐地使你气壮，心里觉得胜利。每回你踏了一步，对你的脚你会有些敬意。伞拿在手中像个咆哮的战利品。

我们走到乡下了：雨雾过去了；我们碰着我们的老朋友，更夫们，他们大概是身体肥重，态度安闲，什么也不关心样子，整个人衣衫的成分比身体还多，好像想什么，实在并不想什么东西，年纪很老而不会叫人见而生敬，一点用处也没有。不，他们不是没用，因为住在屋里人想他们是很中用的，他们的用处也就在给人以这种思想。我们并不像往常那样可怜更夫。老年人多半不注意按时的睡眠。他们在床上或者还睡不着，可是在床上他们不能够挣钱。他们所能得的睡眠或者因为是在更棚里偷偷地得来的，特别甜蜜；他们自己觉得很重要，对住户有各种特权，还加上他们的大氅同更棚，难怪他们自视是个"人物"。他们在个人职业外，加上这公家的职务。汤金斯同他们一

---

5 "somebody": a person of importance 要人。

is a cobbler as well as they, but then he is no watchman. He cannot speak to "things of night", nor bid "any man stand in the King's name".[1] He does not get fees and gratitude from the old, the infirm, and the drunken; nor "let gentlemen go"; nor is he "a parish-man". The churchwardens don't speak to him. If he put himself over so much in the way[2] of "the great plumber", he would not say "How do you find yourself, Tomkins?"—"An ancient and quiet watchman"[3]. Such he was in the time of Shakespeare, and such he is now. Ancient, because he cannot help it; and quiet, because he will not help it, if possible; his object being to procure quiet on all sides, his own included[4]. For this reason, he does not make too much noise in crying the hour, nor is offensively particular[5] in his articulation. No man shall sleep the worse for him, out of a horrid sense of the word "three". The sound shall be three, four, or one, as suits their mutual convenience[6].

Yet characters are to be found even among watchmen. They are

---

1 any man stand in the King's name: 更夫晚上遇着行人，就用这句话叫他站住，盘问后才放他走。

2 put himself... in the way: put himself in a position to call.

3 an ancient and quiet watchman: 在莎士比亚所著的《亨利第六世》(*Henry VI*) 第三部第四幕中，有一个角色是更夫，莎士比亚说他是 "an ancient and quiet watchman"。

4 his own included: 他的责任既然是保守安静，自己自然不好闹得很利害。

5 particular: clear.

样做补鞋匠，但是他却不是更夫。他不能够谈"夜里的事情"，也不能"用皇上的名字叫谁站住"。他没有得老人家，孱弱的同醉汉的小钱同感谢；没有说，"让先生们走过罢"；他不是"教区的人员"。教堂里的执事不对他说话。不管他如何常排在这"大洋铁匠"面前，他绝不会问，"汤金斯，你好吗？"——"一个老年安静的更夫"。莎士比亚时代，更夫是这样，现在更夫还是这样。老年，因为他没有法子能够不老；安静，若使能够不安静，他也不愿意；他的目的是要办到四处都是寂寂地安宁，他自己的心也包括在内。所以他叫钟点并不叫得太大声，也不故意捣乱地说得太清楚。没有一个人会真听到叫"三"点，心里害怕，睡得不稳。他说的声音，听的人们觉得怎么解释才合式，就可那样解释，三点，四点，一点都行。

就是更夫里也有性格的分别。他们不只是大氅，笨大的躯

---

6 mutual convenience：更夫麻麻糊糊地叫点，听的人爱把它当几点，就可以当作几点，岂不是个双方都方便的事。

not all mere coat, and lump, and indifference. By the way, what do they think of in general? How do they vary the monotony of their ruminations from one to two, and from two to three, and so on? Are they comparing themselves with the unofficial cobbler; thinking of what they shall have for dinner tomorrow; or what they were about six years ago; or that their lot is the hardest in the world (as insipid old people are apt to think, for the pleasure of grumbling[1]); or that it has some advantages nevertheless, besides fees; and that if they are not in bed, their wife is?

Of characters, or rather varieties among watchmen, we remember several. One was a Dandy Watchman, who used to ply at the top of Oxford Street, next the park. We called him the dandy, on account of his utterance[2]. He had a mincing way with it, pronouncing the a in the word "past" as it is in hat, —making a little preparatory hem before he spoke, and then bringing out his "Păst ten" in a style of genteel indifference[3], as if, upon the whole, he was of that opinion.

Another was the Metallic Watchman, who paced the same street towards Hanover Square, and had a clang in his voice like a

---

1 for the pleasure of grumbling: 活画出老头子的精神，不是什么不舒服，才发牢骚，因为爱说牢骚话，方去找些理由来。

2 on account of his utterance: 纨袴〔绔〕子弟，时髦人物说话时故意装出一种特别腔调。

3 genteel indifference: 时髦人爱排出无精打彩〔采〕，什么事也不足关心的样子给人看，以显他是个超乎一切的脚色。

体同满不关心的神情。却说,他们普通所想的是什么呢?他们由一点钟到两点,两点到三点一直下去,怎么样来变换他思想的单调呢?他们是不是把自己同没当差事的补鞋匠比较;想明天午餐吃的是什么东西;回忆六年前自己的情形;嗟叹他们的命运是世上最苦的(无聊的老人常爱这样想,为的因此可以享那发牢骚的快乐);或者想起在小钱外还有别的利益;安慰自己,他们虽然不在床上,他们的老妻却安歇着?

关于更夫的特别性格,或者说不同的性格还好些,我记得几个。一个"公子式的更夫",他在牛津街公园邻近走来走去。我们称他是公子,为的他说话的声音与众不同。他说话半吞半吐,past这字中间的a当hat这字中间的a念——说话以前,先预备地咳一下,等一会才说出他的"过——了——十——点",那文雅地不留心样子,好像只讲他也觉是这时光罢。

另一个是铁打的更夫,他也在牛津街向着汉诺瓦广场巡行,他声音似喇叭的响亮。他除声音外没有别的奇特处,不过在更

trumpet. He was a voice and nothing else[1]; but any difference is something in a watchman.

A third, who cried the hour in Bedford Square, was remarkable in his calling for being abrupt and loud. There was a fashion among his tribe just come up[2] at that time, of omitting the words "past" and "o'clock", and crying only the number of the hour. I know not whether a recollection I have of his performance one night is entire matter of fact[3], or whether any subsequent fancies of what might have taken place are mixed up with it; but my impression is, that as I was turning the corner into the square with a friend, and was in the midst of a discussion in which numbers were concerned, we were suddenly startled, as if in solution of it, by a brief and tremendous outcry of—ONE[4]. This paragraph ought to have been at the bottom of the page, and the word printed a bruptly around the corner.

A fourth watchman was a very singular phenomenon[5], a Reading Watchman. He had a book, which he read by the light of his lantern; and instead of a pleasant, gave you a very uncomfortable idea of him. It seemed cruel to pitch amidst so many discomforts and privations one who had imagination enough to wish to be relieved from

---

1 nothing else: 他除声音之外, 别的都很平常, 没有出奇的地方。
2 come up: become fashionable.
3 matter of fact: real fact.

夫有一些特别处，也就算难得了。

第三个是在柏底福广场叫更的，他的叫声简短洪大得奇怪。那时候他们这班人有一种新时髦，就是略去"过了"和"点钟"几个字，只唤出数目来。我不知道我对从前一个晚上事情的记忆是完全事实，还有没有我以后想像为可能的成分杂些进去；不过我的印象是当我同一位同学在基角拐湾〔弯〕到广场的时候，正在谈论个同数目有关系的问题，我们忽然好像得到答案地，给一个简短颤动的叫声——壹——吓着了。这一段应当放在页底，这个"壹"字也当突然地印在纸角上。

第四个更夫是一个非常特别的怪人，一个看书的更夫。他有一本书，借他灯笼的光念着；可是他不能给你快感，反使你替他难过。将一个居然有想像力打算赶丢愁闷的人搁在这许多

---

4 "one"：叫更时说的一点。
5 phenomenon：remarkable person 奇人。

them. Nothing but a sluggish vacuity¹ befits a watchman.

But the oddest of all was the *Sliding* Watchman. Think of walking up a street in the depth of a frosty winter², with long ice in the gutters, and sleet over head, and then figure to yourself a sort of bale of a man in white, coming sliding towards you with a lantern in one hand, and an umbrella over his head. It was the oddest mixture of luxury and hardship, of juvenility and old age! But this looked agreeable. Animal spirits³ carry everything before them; and our invincible friend seemed a watchman for Rabelais⁴. Time was run at and butted by him like a goat⁵. The slide seemed to bear him half through the night at once; he slipped from out of his box and his common-places at one rush of a merry thought, and seemed to say, "Everything's in imagination; —here goes⁶ the whole weight of my office."

But we approach our home. How still the trees! How deliciously asleep the country! How beautifully grim and nocturnal this

---

1 sluggish vacuity：头脑空虚，毫无思想的人一定举动甚慢。所以这两字合起来成一个 phrase。

2 the depth of a frosty winter：the most wintry part 严冬。

3 animal spirits：liveliness of disposition.（spirits 作此解时，常居复数。）

4 Rabelais：十六世纪法国文学家，他最善滑稽同讥讽，荒诞不经的故事，来作外表；这个更夫浪漫古怪，所以说配放在 Rabelais 书里。

5 time was run at and butted by him like a goat：他溜来溜去一下，时间

困苦缺乏之中，真像件残忍事情。只有一种懒洋洋毫无思想的样子，才同更夫合式。

但是最古怪的是一个溜行的更夫。试想一下在严霜深冬的道上走着，沟里有长条的冰，上面雨雪霏霏，再画一个像白袋子的人，手里拿个灯笼，遮着雨伞，向你滑溜过来。这是苦工同享乐，青春和老年最奇异的混在一块！但是这种结合使人看得高兴。什么事只要能够带劲有彩就好；我们这壮健不屈的更夫到〔倒〕似拉伯立书里的人物。"时间"像个山羊给他赶得东奔西跑。他这一溜仿佛可以溜过整个半夜；他兴致一来，就由他的更棚同那陈腐的势力里溜出，好像在那里说，"什么事情全靠着心境；——现在我这职务的全部压迫一些也没有了。"

可是我们走近家了。树林多么寂静！旷野睡得多么甜蜜！这条望上走的花径配着那寒冷的白色天空，现出多么美丽地严

就过去了，所以说时间好像是个羊，给他赶得东跑西奔了。

6 goes: disappears.

wooded avenue of ascent, against the cold white sky! The watchmen and patrols, which the careful citizens have planted in abundance within a mile of their doors, salute us with their "good mornings"; — not so welcome as we pretend[1], for we ought not to be out so late; and it is one of the assumptions[2] of these fatherly old fellows to remind us of it. Some fowls, who have made a strange roost in a tree, flutter as we pass them; —another pull up[3] the hill, unyielding; a few strides on a level; and there is the light in the window, the eye of the warm soul of the house, —one's home. How particular, and yet how universal, is that word[4]; and how surely does it deposit every one for himself in his own nest!

---

1 pretend: take them to be.
2 assumption: presumption.
3 pull up: stop on.
4 how particular, and yet how universal, is that word: 各人的家庭不同，所以说起家庭，各人有他自己的观念，但是我们由家庭所得的安慰是非常普遍的，天伦之乐，谁也是一样的。

肃又含着夜色！小心的居民安置在离他们大门一里路内的好多更夫同巡查向我们祝"早安"；——这句话没有我们有意把它当做的那么客气，因为我们不该在外面逛得这么迟；这班像父亲式的老头子擅自拿这句带讥讽话来提醒我们。有的家禽本来很奇怪地栖在树上，我们走过时鼓翼飞去；——别的站在山上，毫不退让；还有几个在平地上跨行；在那个地方，那个同我们有特别关系的窗子里有那个我们所熟识的光，那是屋里恳挚亲爱的人的眼睛——人们的家庭。家庭，这个字对每人所引起的感想是多么不同，然而又多么普遍地感动人心；它是多么一些不错地将每个人安放在他自己的巢窝里！

Logan Pearsall Smith

(1865—)[1]

The Rose

The old lady had always been proud of the great rose-tree in her garden, and was fond of telling how it had grown from a cutting[2] she had brought years before from Italy, when she was first married. She and her husband had been travelling back in their carriage from Rome (it was before the time of railways), and on a bad piece of road south of Siena they had broken down, and had been forced to pass the night in a little house by the roadside. The accommodation was wretched of course; she had spent a sleepless night, and rising early had stood, wrapped up, at her window, with the cool air blowing on her face, to watch the dawn. She could still, after all these years, remember the blue mountains with the bright moon above them, and

---

1 作者逝于1946年。——编者注

玫 瑰 树

这位老太太对她园里那株大玫瑰树总是很自夸,老爱说给人听,这株树是怎样由一个砍下的枝干长大的,那枝干是在好几年以前由意大利带回来的,当她才结婚时候。她同她的丈夫坐马车由罗马回来(这是在发明火车时期以前),在丝莺娜南边一块不好的道路上,他们的车子坏了,他们不得不在路旁一个小屋里过夜。房里的设备自然是很麻糊;她整夜没有睡好觉,很早就起来,围着东西,站在窗前看朝阳,那时凉风向她脸上吹着。经过了这许多年,她还记得那明月底下的青山,同怎么

---

2 cutting: a slip.

how a far-off town on one of the peaks had gradually grown whiter and whiter, till the moon faded, the mountains were touched[1] with the pink of the rising sun, and suddenly the town was lit as by an illumination, one window after another catching and reflecting the sun's beams, till at last the whole little city twinkled and sparkled up in the sky like a nest of stars.

That morning, finding they would have to wait while their carriage was being repaired, they had driven in a local conveyance up to the city on the mountain, where they had been told they would find better quarters; and there they had stayed two or three days. It was one of the miniature Italian cities with a high church, a pretentious piazza, a few narrow streets and little palaces, perched, all compact and complete, on the top of a mountain, within an enclosure of walls hardly larger than an English kitchen garden[2]. But it was full of life and noise, echoing all day and all night with the sounds of feet and voices.

The Café[3] of the simple inn where they stayed was the meeting-place of the notabilities of the little city; the *Sindaco*, the *avvocato*, the doctor, and a few others; and among them they noticed a beautiful, slim, talkative old man, with bright black eyes and snowwhite

---

1 touched: illumined.
2 kitchen garden: 大菜园。
3 Café: a restaurant.

样在很远一个山峰上的城镇渐渐地变成白色，等到月亮看不见了，那高山给上升的太阳的红光照着，忽然间那城镇像点着火地发光起来，一个窗户跟着一个窗户抓到，又反射出去太阳的光线，最后全城在空中闪烁着，辉煌着像一窝的明星。

那早上，知道当他们马车正在修理时候他们要等着，他们就坐地方用的车到山上那个城镇去，据说在那里他们可以得到更好的住所；在那里他们就滞留两三天。这是意大利小城之一，有高耸的礼拜堂，傲慢自得的大方场，几条狭窄的街道同几处小小的宫殿，整整齐齐稠密地栖止在山颠上，城墙围着一块比英国菜园大不得多少的地方。但是这城是充满了生命同嘈杂，整天整夜地回应出人们脚步同说话的声音。

他们所住的那个简朴小旅馆的咖啡室是那小城里名人聚会地方；市长，律师，医生同几个做旁的事情人；他们注意到里头有一位面貌秀美，身体瘦长的好说话老人，一对发光的黑眼

hair—tall and straight and still with the figure of a youth, although the waiter told them with pride that the *Conte was molto vecchio*— would in fact be eighty in the following year. He was the last of his family, the water added—they had once been great and rich people— but he had no descendants; in fact the waiter mentioned with complacency[1], as if it were a story on which the locality prided itself, that the Conte had been unfortunate in love, and had never married.

The old gentleman, however, seemed cheerful enough; and it was plain that he took an interest in the strangers, and wished to make their acquaintance. This was soon effected by the friendly waiter; and after a little talk the old man invited them to visit his villa and garden which were just outside the walls of the town. So the next afternoon, when the sun began to descend, and they saw in glimpses through doorways and windows, blue shadows beginning to spread over the brown mountains, they went to pay their visit. It was not much of a place[2], a small, modernised, stucco villa, with a hot pebbly garden, and in it a stone basin with torpid gold fish, and a statue of Diana[3] and her hounds against the wall. But what gave a glory to it was a gigantic rose-tree which clambered over the house, almost smothering the windows, and filling the air with the perfume

---

1 complacency: satisfaction.
2 much of a place: big place.
3 Diana：月神（希腊神话：月神爱打猎，所以她像旁有猎狗）。

睛，雪白头发——体格高而直，还带着少年的态度，虽然那侍者很得意地告诉他们这位伯爵是个年纪很大的老人——真的，第二年就要八十岁了。他是他家里最后剩下来的一个人，侍者继续着说——他家从前是很有声望，很富的，——但是他没有子孙；真的，那侍者很愉快地说，好像这是个那地方人民觉得很荣耀的故事，说这位伯爵曾经失恋过，从来没有结婚。

　　但是，那老绅士却很高兴样子；一看就知道，他对于生人感觉有趣味，想和他们认识。这个和蔼的侍者立刻替他将这事办好，谈了一会，这老人请他们到他的别墅同花园去逛，那是正在城镇的城墙外面。所以第二天下午当太阳开始下降，他们由门口窗口瞥见棕色的山上已经有蓝的影子在那里开展着时候，他们去拜会他。那别墅并不大，一个近代式石灰墙的小别墅，连着一座铺着石卵的花园，里面有一个石池，养些无精打采的金鱼，还有一个月神像，旁边刻着她的猎狗，都靠着围墙。但是使这个园光荣显赫的是一株伟大玫瑰树，这树爬到房子上面，差不多把窗口塞满，使空气充满了她的芬香。当他们赞美这树

of its sweetness. Yes, it was a fine rose, the Conte said proudly when they praised it, and he would tell the Signora about it. And as they sat there, drinking the wine he offered them, he alluded with the cheerful indifference of old age to his love affair, as though he took for granted[1] that they had heard of it already.

"The lady lived across the valley there beyond that hill. I was a young man then, for it was many years ago. I used to ride over to see her; it was a long way, but I rode fast, for young men, as no doubt the Signora knows, are impatient. But the lady was not kind, she would keep me waiting, oh, for hours; and one day when I had waited very long I grew very angry, and as I walked up and down in the garden where she had told me she would see me, I broke one of her roses, broke a branch from it; and when I saw what I had done, I hid it inside my coat—so—[2]; and when I came home I planted it, and the Signora sees how it has grown. If the Signora admires it, I must give her a cutting to plant also in her garden; I am told the English have beautiful gardens that are green, and not burnt with the sun like ours."[3]

The next day, when their mended carriage had come up to fetch

---

1　took for granted: assumed.
2　"— so —"：当时那位老绅士，做出他从前隐存花枝的样子给她看，一边口里说"——这样子——"。

的时候，伯爵得意地说，这确是一株好玫瑰树，他要同这位太太谈这株玫瑰的故事。当他们坐在那里，饮那他请他们喝的酒时候，他用种老年人快乐的不关心态度提到他的情史，那随便的样子，仿佛他以为他们已经听过了。

"那位姑娘住在那山过去的谷里。那时我是个青年，因为这是好些年前的事情。我常常骑马去会她；路是很长，但是我骑得很快，因为年青人总是性急，这点太太一定知道。然而那姑娘心肠很硬，她要让我等，啊，好几个钟头；有一天我等得好久，生气了，当我在那她告诉我她要会我的园中踱来踱去的时候，我折断她的玫瑰，折了一枝下来；当我看清我所做的事情，我把这枝存在我衣服里面——像这样子——；我回家时，就将这枝栽下，太太，你看现在长得多大了。若使太太赞美这玫瑰，我一定要送她一枝，也栽在她的花园里；我听说英国有美丽绿色的花园，不像我们这给太阳烧焦了的花园。"

第二天当他们修理好了的马车来接他们，他们正开始由旅

---

3 not burnt with the sun like ours：意大利居欧洲的南部，天气暖和，晴时甚多，不像英国那么常下雨。

them, and they were just starting to drive away from the inn, the Conte's old servant appeared with the rose-cutting neatly wrapped up, and the compliments and wishes for a *buon viaggio* from her master. The town collected to see them depart, and the children ran after their carriage through the gate of the little city. They heard a rush of feet behind them for a few moments, but soon they were far down toward the valley; the little town with all its noise and life was high above them on its mountain peak.

She had planted the rose at home, where it had grown and flourished in a wonderful manner; and every June the great mass of leaves and shoots still broke out into a passionate splendour of scent and crimson colour, as if in its root and fibres there still burnt the anger and thwarted desire of that Italian lover. Of course the old Conte must have died many years ago; she had forgotten his name, and had even forgotten the name of the mountain city that she had stayed in, after first seeing it twinkling at dawn in the sky, like a nest of stars.

馆出发的时候，伯爵的老仆人拿着清清楚楚包好的折下来的玫瑰枝走来，说她主人祝他们一路快活平安。镇里人聚集着看他们出发，小孩们跟着马车跑，跑过小城的城门。起先他们听见后面有匆忙脚步的声音，但是不久他们深深进到山谷里面了；那小城同里头所包含的嘈杂和生命是高高地站在那山颠。

　　她将这玫瑰栽住家里，这树老是生长发达得奇怪；每年六月时候，那一大堆的枝叶还是送出充满香气同红色的热情华丽气象，好像在树根树心里还燃烧着这位意大利爱人的愤怒同失望。自然，这位老伯爵一定是死了好几年了；她忘却他的名字，而且起先在早上看见在空中闪烁着像一窝的明星，后来她住在里面的那个山上小城，她也忘记是叫做什么名字了。

W. H. Hudson
(1841—1922)

The Samphire Gatherer

At sunset, when the strong wind from the sea was beginning to feel cold[1], I stood on the top of the sand-hill looking down at an old woman hurrying about over the low damp ground beneath—a bit of sea-flat divided from the sea by the ridge of sand; and I wondered at her, because her figure was that of a feeble old woman, yet she moved—I had almost said flitted—over that damp level ground in a surprisingly swift light manner, pausing at intervals to stoop and gather something from the surface. But I couldn't see her distinctly enough to satisfy myself[2]; the sun was sinking below the horizon, and that dimness in the air and coldness in the wind at day's decline,

---

1 to feel cold: to make one feel cold.

采集海草之人

　　太阳下山时候，海里吹来的烈风开始使人感觉到寒冷，我站在个沙邱顶上，看底下一个老妇人在低湿的地上匆忙的走来走去——那是一块近海的平地，隔个沙陂就是海；我心里觉得很奇怪，因为她的样子是个衰弱的老妇人，但是她走动——我差不要说，飞动——过那平湿地面的样子是轻快得出奇，有时停住弯下腰，由地面检〔捡〕些东西。可是我不能够看得很清楚，使我自己满足：太阳正落到水平线下，空气的朦胧同日暮

---

2 to satisfy myself: to attain to conviction.

when the year too was declining¹ made all objects book dim. Going down to her I found that she was old, with thin grey hair on an uncovered head, a lean dark face with regular features and grey eyes that were not old and looked steadily at mine, affecting me with a sudden mysterious sadness. For they were unsmiling eyes and themselves expressed an unutterable sadness, as it appeared to me at the first swift glance; or perhaps not that, as it presently seemed, but a shadowy something which sadness had left in them, when all pleasure and all interest in life forsook her, with all affections, and she no longer cherished either memories or hopes². This may be nothing but conjecture or fancy, but if she had been a visitor from another world³ she could not have seemed more strange to me.

I asked her what she was doing there so late in the day, and she answered in a quiet even voice which had a shadow⁴ in it too, that she was gathering samphire of that kind which grows on the flat saltings and has a dull green leek-like fleshy leaf. At this season, she informed me, it was fit for gathering to pickle and put by for use during the year. She carried a pail to put it in, and a table-knife in her hand to dig the plants up by the roots, and she also had an old sack in which she put every dry stick and chip of wood she came across.

---

1 declining：前面用 day's decline，此处又用 declining，重复得有趣。
2 she no longer... or hopes：请参看本书110页"the complacent retrospect of past joys and hopes"注。

的冷风,当这又是年暮时候,把一切东西都弄模糊了。走下到她那里,我看出她是个老年人,没有带〔戴〕帽子的头上有稀少灰白的头发,脸孔瘦黑,形容端正,灰色的眼睛并显不出老气,不动地瞧着我,她这种神情使我忽然间感到一种莫名其妙的悲哀。因为那是没有笑容的眼睛,表现出一种说不出的悲情,头一下瞥见时,我是这样觉得;或者她现在并不悲哀,那不过是悲哀留下在眼睛里的一个影子,当一切人生的快乐同兴趣,跟着一切的情感全舍她了,她也不再怀着什么回忆同希望了。这或者只是我的瞎猜同幻想,但是若使她是个由别一世界来的人,我也不会觉得更奇怪。

我问她这么迟时候在那儿干什么,她用种悄悄地没有什么高低的声音(那声音里也带了影子)回答说她是采集那生在平坦盐泽的海草,那草的叶子像葱,暗绿色,汁很多。她告诉我这时节刚好采集腌着,搁起来整年都可以用。她带个桶子来装这草,手里拿一把餐刀,把小树连根掘起,他〔她〕还有一个

---

3 a visitor from another world: a ghost.
4 a shadow:声音里面带有细微凄惨的调。

She added that she had gathered samphire at this same spot every August end for very many years.

I prolonged the conversation, questioning her and listening with affected interest to her mechanical answers, while trying to fathom[1] those unsmiling, unearthly[2] eyes that looked so steadily at mine.

And presently, as we talked, a babble of human voices reached our ears, and half turning we saw the crowd, or rather procession[3], of golfers[4] coming from the golf-house by the links where they had been drinking tea. Ladies and gentlemen players forty or more of them, following in a loose line; in couples and small groups, on their way to the Golfers' Hotel, a little further up the coast; a remarkably good-looking lot with well-fed happy faces, well dressed and in a merry mood, all freely talking and laughing. Some were staying at the hotel, and for the others a score or so of motorcars were standing before its gates to take them inland to their homes, or to houses where they were staying.

We suspended the conversation while they were passing us, within three yards of where we stood, and as they passed the story of the links where they had been amusing themselves since luncheontime

---

1 to fathom: to comprehend.
2 unearthly: ghostly.
3 procession：那班游客，衣服丽都，像一队艳装的游行者。

旧布袋，她碰着的每条干树枝同柴碎都丢在里头。她还说她每年八月底在这同一地方采海草已经有好多年数了。

我将我们的谈话延长下去，问她许多话，对她那机械式的答话故意做有趣味地听着，同时我却想法去探测这对不含笑容，没有人气，不动地望着我的眼睛。

我们谈不久，一阵嘈杂的人声传到我们耳朵里，我们半转过身来，看见一群（说一队还好些）打棒球人[4]由那沙邱旁边他们吃茶的棒球房里走来。女的同男的打棒球人，四十多个左右，零零落落地，有一对同行，有几人一组，望着那边海滩上的"棒球旅馆"走；这是一群非常漂亮的人物，肥肥的快乐脸孔，衣服很讲究，高兴得很的样子，随随便便谈天说笑。有些在旅馆里住，其余的人，有二十来辆汽车在旅馆门口等着，预备送他们回到内地的家里，或者他们暂住的房子。

当他们在离我们站的地方三码以内走过时候，我们的谈话暂时停止了，他们走后，我心中记起他们午后游玩的那块沙邱

---

4 本文中 golf，梁遇春均译作棒球，故有打棒球人、棒球房、棒球旅馆、棒球场等译名。——编者注

came into my mind. The land there was owned by an old, an ancient, family; they had occupied it, so it is said, since the Conquest[1], but the head of the house was now poor, having no house property in London, no coal mines in Wales, no income from any other source than the land, the twenty or thirty thousand acres let for farming. Even so he would not have been poor, strictly speaking, but for the sons, who preferred a life of pleasure in town, where they probably had private establishments of their own. At all events they kept race-horses[2], and had their cars, and lived in the best clubs, and year by year the patient old father was called upon to discharge their debts of honour[3]. It was a painful position for so estimable a man to be placed in, and he was much pitied by his friends and neighbours, who regarded him as a worthy representative of the best and oldest family in the county. But he was compelled to do what he could to make both ends meet[4], and one of the little things he did was to establish golf-links over a mile or so of sand-hills, lying between the ancient coast village and the sea, and to build and run a Golfers' Hotel[5] in order to attract visitors from all parts. In this way, incidentally, the villagers were cut off from their old direct way to the sea

---

1 the Conquest: the Norman Conquest of England (1066).
2 race-horses: 英国的贵族常养骏马,于赛马时下注和人赌输赢。
3 debts of honour: 没有经过法律手续借的债,因为是以人格担保,

的历史。那块地方是属一个很老的世家；有人说，从诺曼民族征服英国的时候起，他们就占有这块地方；但是这家家长现在穷了，没有房产在伦敦，没有煤矿在威尔士，除租给人耕种的二三万英亩田外，没有别的收入来源。实在说起来，就是这样子他也不会穷，若使没有那班儿子，他们爱城市里的快乐生活，在那里他们或者有私房子。最少，他们养有比赛用的马，自己有汽车，天天在最好的俱乐部过活，年年他们要这忍耐的老父替他们还赌债，把这么可敬的家长处在这样情形中，这真是苦痛的地位，他的朋友邻居都很可怜他，说他是那郡里最好最老的世家的一个好代表。但是他逼到不得不尽他的能力弄成个出入相抵，他因此所干的小事之一就是建设这沙邱上面一英里来长的棒球场，位置在海同沿海的老村中间，还盖座棒球旅馆，吸引各地的来客。这样子偶然地把村里人到海最短的旧路截断

所以叫"名誉的债"，此字现多半指赌债。
    4 to make both ends meet: to live within income.
    5 run a hotel: keep a hotel.

and deprived of those barren dunes, which were their open space and recreation ground and had stood them in the place of a common[1] for long centuries. They were warned off and told that they must use a path to the beach which took them over half a mile from the village. And they had been very humble and obedient and had made no complaint. Indeed, the agent had assured them that they had every reason to be grateful of the overlord, since in return for that trivial inconvenience they had been put to they would have the golfers there, and there would be employment for some of the village boys as caddies. Nevertheless, I had discovered that they were not grateful but considered that an injustice had been done to them, and it rankled in their hearts.

  I remembered all this while the golfers were streaming by[2], and wondered if this poor woman did not, like her fellow-villagers, cherish a secret bitterness against those who had deprived them of the use of the dunes where for generations they had been accustomed to walk or sit or lie on the loose yellow sands among the barren grasses, and had also cut off their direct way to the sea where they went daily in search of bits of firewood and whatever else the waves threw up which would be a help to them in their poor lives.

---

  1 common: 英国于城市，乡村，皆有公地，供人民随便使用，这样的地就叫做 common。
  2 streaming by: going along one after another as the flowing of a stream.

了，那个荒野的沙邱，从前可以算是他们的空地同游戏场，他们当公地用已经好几百年了，现在也由他们手里夺去。人们警告他们，吩咐他们到海岸要用另一条路，那路由乡村走起要走半英里多。而且他们一向是驯良听命，没有露过怨声。真的，那管理田地人要他们相信，他们有许多理由对地主应当感谢，因为偿补他们所受的些须不方便，他们有打棒球人在这里，有些村里小孩会被雇去当拿球棍的差事。然而我看出他们并不感谢，只是以为他们受了人们的欺侮，这件事使他们痛心。

当打棒球人流水般走过时候，我记起这么多事情，心中想不知道这个可怜妇人会不会和她的同村人一样对这班人秘密地怀一种恶感，因为他们剥夺了村人们沙邱的使用权，在那松松的黄沙上面，荒草丛中步行，闲坐或者躺着，村人已经成个习惯好几代了；他们又截断村人到海最近的路，那里村人每天去找些柴同海浪抛上岸的一切东西，这些对他们穷苦的生活都有帮助。

If it be so, I thought, some change will surely come into those unchanging eyes at the sight of all these merry, happy golfers on their way to their hotel and their cars and luxurious homes.

But though I watched her face closely there was no change, no faintest trace of ill-feeling or feeling of any kind, only that same shadow which had been there was there still, and her fixed eyes were like those of a captive bird or animal, that gaze at us, yet seem not to see us but to look through and beyond[1] us. And it was the same when they had all gone by and we finished our talk and I put money in her hand; she thanked me without a smile, in the same quiet even tone of voice in which she had replied to my question about the samphire.

I went up once more to the top of the ridge, and looking down saw her again as I had seen her at first, only dimmer, swiftly, lightly moving or flitting moth-like or ghost-like over the low flat salting, still gathering samphire in the cold wind, and the thought that came to me was that I was looking at and had been interviewing a being that was very like a ghost, or in any case a soul, a something which could not be described, like certain atmospheric effects in earth and

---

1 through and beyond: 形容她眼睛渺茫地什么也不注意，对于客人的衣服等毫不关心，老是那么钉〔盯〕着望，好像要看穿过客人的身子。

我暗自忖着，若使她会存些恶感，那看到这群高兴快乐的打棒球人向着他们的旅馆，汽车同奢华的家庭走时候，这一对不变的眼睛一定会有变化。

但是我虽然很近地注意她的面容，一些变化也没有，就是恶感或者任一情感的顶微痕迹也找不出，只是以前在眼里的悲哀影子还在那里，她那固定的眼睛好像一个囚着的鸟兽的眼睛，注视着我们，然而又不像是看我们，倒是看穿过我们，看到我们背后的东西。他们都走过了，我们也谈完了，我把钱放在她手上，她的神气老是那么样子；她没有笑容地对我道谢，那悄悄地没有什么高低的声音同她答应我问她关于海草时是相同的。

我又走上那山顶，向下望又看她像我起先看她一样，不过更模糊些，轻快地像飞蛾或者像鬼魅行动着或者飞动着，在那低平盐田上面，还在冷风里采取海草，那时我心里想的是，这个我正看见，起先对谈过的人是一个非常像鬼的人，无论如何是一个描写不出的灵魂，像风景画家没法描摹只好置之不理的

water and sky which are ignored[1] by the landscape painter. To protect himself[2] he cultivates what is called the "sloth of the eye": he thrusts his fingers into his ears, so to speak, not to hear that mocking voice that follows and mocks him with his miserable limitations. He who seeks to convey his impressions with a pen is almost as badly off[3]: the most he can do in such instances as the one related, is to endeavour to convey the emotion evoked by what he has witnessed.

Let me then take the case of the man who has trained his eyes, or rather whose vision has unconsciously trained itself, to look at every face he meets, to find in most cases something, however little, or the person's inner life. Such a man could hardly walk the length of the Strand and Fleet Street or of Oxford Street without being startled at the sight of a face which haunts him with its tragedy, its mystery, the strange things it has half revealed. But it does not haunt[4] him long; another arresting[5] face follows, and then another, and the impressions all fade and vanish from the memory in a little while. But from time to time, at long intervals, once perhaps in a lustrum, he will encounter a face that will not cease to haunt him, whose

---

1 ignored: intentionally neglected.
2 to protect himself: 因为看到美妙的东西，又画不出来是件非常难过的事情，到〔倒〕不如装傻假盲，免得自己受苦。
3 badly off: unsuccessful; miserable.
4 haunt: 含有"常来和他捣乱"的意思。

一种水天大地所生的空气气象一样。为自卫起见，风景画家练出一种本领，叫做"眼力的迟钝"：可以说他用手指塞着耳朵，免得听到那跟着他，讥笑他可怜的有限能力的嘲笑声音。用笔来传达印象的人是差不多同样地不能成功：像上面所说这件事，尽他力之所能只是努力将他当时心中所引起的情感传达出来。

让我现在说一种人，他练习他的眼睛，（不如说他的眼力不知不觉里自己练习，）他要由他所碰的多数脸孔里去探出些他们的内心生活，不管多么微小。这样人不能够走完司特能街同弗立街或者奥士福街，而不很惊奇地遇着一种脸孔，那里面所包含的悲剧同神秘分子和那半露出的奇怪消息会缠绕他的心中。但是这印象不会盘占他的思想很久；另外一个使他不得不注意的脸孔跟着来，一会儿又有一个，这么多的印象不久却全由记忆里消散去了。可是有时，隔了好久时间，或者五年一回，他会逢着一个脸孔，老是缠绕他心中，那显明的印象好几年都不

---

5 arresting: impressive.

vivid impression will not fade for years. It was face and eyes of that kind which I met in the samphire gatherer on that cold evening; but the mystery of it is a mystery still[1].

---

1 the mystery of it is a mystery still：此句结束全篇，使读者感到有悠然不尽之意。当代小品作家和十八九世纪小品作家不同的地方，在于从前作者常把话说得清楚明白，现在许多小品作家却多在涵〔含〕蓄这点下功夫，使他们的作品耐人寻味。这还是近代文学的普通趋向，便于 suggestive 这点，什么话只说半句，其余让聪明的读者自己去领会。散文如此，近代诗也是如是，所以近代诗特别讲究音乐和印象。因为这两样东西最富有 suggestive 能力。但是十八世纪小品那样纯练精净的恰到好处和十九世纪小品那种痛快淋漓，一泻千丈的气魄，都有它们千古不磨的价值。当代小品文家的作风不过是想另外开一条路，我们可以把它们看做美的种类不同的作品。这不过是概括地说，其中各人有自己的风格，千殊万变，有待个别的研究，而且也不是我这样对近代小品文学涉猎不多的人所能够详细讨论。

会丢失。这种脸孔同眼睛和我那清冷的黄昏所碰的采集海草的女人是同类的；但是那里面的神秘始终还是个神秘。

Robert Lynd
(1879—　)[1]

This Body

There are occasional items of news in the papers that pull us up[2] and tempt us to examine our attitude in regard to some question as if for the first time. One item of the kind was the announcement of the will of Edward Martyn, Irish revivalist and cousin of Mr. George Moore[3] in accordance with which[4] his dead body was to be given to a medical school for dissection and the remains were afterwards to be buried, like other dissecting-room corpses, in a pauper's grave. Who, on reading this, could fail to turn round[5] and ask himself whether he could endure the prospect of his body's being

---

1　作者逝于1949年。——编者注
2　pull us up: check us from reading onward.
3　Mr. George Moore: 爱尔兰独立运动者，他又是一个小说家兼批评

躯　　体

报纸里偶然有些新闻使我们看时停住,引起我们去考察我们关于一个问题的态度,好像这是第一次才想到的样子。这类新闻的一个是爱多利亚·马丁遗嘱的公布,他是爱尔兰独立运动者,乔治·摩尔的表兄弟,照他的遗嘱,他的尸体要给一个医学校做解剖用,剩下的同别个解剖过的死尸一样将来埋在贫民冢里。谁念了这段,不会转过来问他自己能不能忍受他身体

家,为英国的一个当代文豪。
   4　which: the will.
   5　to turn round: to face about.

subjected, though past sense, to the knives of medical students? There are few people, indeed, who could be entirely indifferent on such a matter. If a man is careless of the fate of his body after death, as Socarates was, it is thought a sufficiently remarkable fact to be preserved in his biography. Christians ought, perhaps, of all people to have been most able to achieve this happy carelessness. [1]But even the belief in the immortality of the soul has seldom persuaded human beings that a dead body is as worthless as the husk of a seed that has burst out of darkness into a flower. In the result, Christians have for centuries paid honour to dead bodies as though they were more noble than the living, and many a poor man has never had the hats of passers-by raised to him till he has driven through the streets as a corpse[2]. I do not know how far modern Christians believe that after long ages at the sound of a trumpet[3] the body that has been the prey of worms and of dusty time will actually rise out of the earth, recomposed into the likeness of a living man. Probably there are few

---

1 Christians ought, ... happy carelessness.：基督教徒相信灵魂不灭，肉体不过是暂时的皮囊，所以应当看轻躯体才是。

2 paid honour to dead bodies... as a corpse：英人凡是在路上遇着出葬，不管死的是王公大人或者是乞丐奴仆，都是一样地脱帽致敬。小品文学家Alexander Smith在他小品集《梦乡》(*Dreamthorp*) 里面有一篇《死和死的恐惧》(On Death and the Fear of Dying)，就拿这件事来证明死有种神秘能力，把人们的位置提高，他说："Death makes the meanest beggar august, and that augustness would assert itself in the presence of a king." Smith这篇论死的

被医学生拿去开刀（虽然已经没有知觉了）的结局？真的，只有几个人对这事能够毫不关心。若使一个人对他死后躯体的际遇，一些也不留意，像苏格拉底一样，人们想这是一件奇特的事，值得记进他的传里。在一切人们里基督教徒或者应当最容易达到这种快乐的洒脱心境。但是就是灵魂不灭的信仰也很不容易使人们把死尸看做同已由黑暗爆出花了的外壳一样地不值钱。以至于基督教徒一向好几百年对死体表示敬意，好似死体比活人要高贵些，好多穷人从来没有路人向他脱帽，要等到变成死体由街上过去时候，才有人对他致敬。在好多年代之后，那久已做了蛆虫同时间的捕获品的躯体，一听到号筒声音，会真真地由地下起来，再合成像个生人，对这种思想，我不知道现在基督教徒相信的程度有多少。或者现在没有几个人会坚决

小品是他最得意之作，也是关于死的一篇千古绝妙的文章，想研究"人死观"的人，不可不拿来细细咀嚼一番。Smith最爱说死的性质，差不多没有一篇文章不说到死，他只活三十多岁就短命地死了，所以有人以为有谶兆的。

3 the sound of a trumpet：基督教徒相信在世界末日时候，喇叭一吹，死的都由坟墓里出来，受最后的审判，好人就升天堂去。

who would now confess to any certainty about the matter. But many good men in the past believe that the dead body, far from being a worthless garment that the soul had cast off for ever, was the very garment that the soul would resume on its exaltation into Paradise. Even those Christians who despised the body alive glorified it in death[1], and a saint's body that he had kept starved and unclean as beneath contempt was revered after death as something with a divine power to perform miracles. This may seem, and is, paradoxical, but the awe of the living in presence of a dead body is natural to reflecting men. Certain savages, we are told, pay honour to the bodies of the dead only because they fear that, if they do not, the spirits of the dead will haunt them. But the civilised man, who has no such terrors, is as reverent because, perhaps, he sees in the dead body a sign and wonder that changes the aspect of the world for him and brings him to the very door of the mystery of his own life[2].

Whatever be the reason, the world has not yet outgrown the feeling that the dead must be honoured and not treated as refuse. The outcry during the War against the supposed German "corpse-factory", in which dead soldiers were turned into useful oils or chemicals for the munition factories, was something more than an

---

1 despised the body... in death: 有一部分基督教徒极端地鄙弃肉体，以为是阻止灵魂向上的东西，是灵魂的囚狱，可是他死后，人们或者偶像地崇拜他，以为他的一毛一发都具有神秘的能力了。

地说出关于这事的意见。但是从前许多人相信死体绝不是灵魂永远丢下的无用衣服，而是灵魂升到天堂时所要穿的衣服。就是那班看不起活的肉体的基督教徒，对死了的肉体却很尊敬，一个圣人生时饿他的身体，也不把它收拾干净，以为是个连鄙视都不值得的东西，他死后的躯体，人们却崇敬得像包含有神圣力量，能做神迹的东西宝贝。这事看起〈来〉有些，实在是，很反常，但是活人站在死人面前所生的敬畏情绪，凡有反省能力的人自然会有的。我们听说有些野蛮人对死人的肢体表示敬意，是怕不是这样，死会跟他们捣乱。但是没有这种恐惧的文明人也是同样地尊敬死体，或者因为他在死体上看到一种预兆，一件奇事，把他世界的外状变化，带他一直到他自己生命神秘的门前。

不管是根据什么理由，世人心里还是觉得死人应当受人尊重，不该像废物一样看待。大战时候，人们以为德国有种"死尸工厂"，在里面将死的兵士化作有用的油或者化学原料供给军

---

2 the very door of the mystery of his own life：死是人生之谜的中心点，只要对于死的性质能够明了，我们也可以看透人生的真相了。

expression of propagandist hypocrisy[1]. It was absurd to believe that the Germans, being human beings, would sanction such a thing, but it was natural to believe that; if they did, they would themselves be so much the less human beings. And yet, if it is right to use a dead man's body for purposes of medicine, there is no logical reason why it should be a crime to use a dead man's body for purposes of war. It is arguable, indeed, that the needs of war are the more urgent, and that therefore the "corpse-factory" should be less horrifying to us than the dissecting-room. As a matter of fact, the dissecting-room would horrify us a great deal more if it were not that we have nationalised (or municipalised) the bodies of friendless paupers[2]. When anatomists sent their scouts into the graveyards to dig up the dead who had died solvent[3], the friends of the dead leagued themselves together and guarded the body by night till it had rotted in the earth. How many of us in our childhood grew up amid a thousand-and-one tales[4] of body-snatchers! What devils they and the kidnappers seemed! How thrilling to hear of their adventures! We might laugh

---

1 propagandist hypocrisy: 要宣传旁人的坏处，自己免不了要假装做个神经锐敏，慈善为怀的君子。

2 the bodies of friendless paupers: 英国没有亲友的穷人死后，尸体给政府拿去，发给医学校做解剖之用。

3 who had died solvent: 死时把债还得清清楚楚，和前面的 paupers 相对照。

械厂用，那种大声疾呼的反对不单是宣传反德者的假仁假义的表现。德国人也是人，我们若使去相信他们居然许可干这事情，这相信当然是太荒诞了；但他们若使真办了这事，我们自然会相信他们没有什么人性。可是，倘然为医学的目的，用死人的肢体是没有错的，我们找不出一个合乎逻辑的理由为什么为战争目的，用死人的肢体，就成个罪恶。真的，还可以这样辩驳说战争的需要是更急迫的，所以"死尸工厂"对我们应当没有解剖室那么可怕。其实，解剖室会把我们吓得更利害，若使我们没有将那无亲无友的穷人躯体拿来算做国家的（或者市区的）公物。当解剖家送他们的喽啰到墓地去掘那死时债还得清清楚楚的死人时候，死人的朋友大家联合起来，晚上守着那死尸，一直等它在土里腐朽了才止。我们多少人幼年时光是在一千零一个偷尸故事的空气里长大的！这般偷尸人同拐子是多么像魔鬼！听到他们的冒险是多么惊心动魄！我们可以像听蓝胡子的

---

4 a thousand-and-one tales：《天方夜谈》是含有一千零一个的故事，所以我们说故事很多时，就说有一千零一个。

at them, as at the crimes of Bluebeard[1], but we laughed uneasily. Yet in another thousand years men may be looking back on the body-snatchers and kidnappers as among the saints of science, and Burke and Hare[2] may be honoured as martyrs. I do not think they will, but it is possible at least that science progressed as a result of their crimes. There is certainly as much to be said in reason for allowing the dissecting-room to choose its bodies casually from the grave-yards as for giving it the right to use its lancets on the unclimed bodies of paupers. But, as most of us hope that neither we nor our friends will end even in these costly days in the workhouse[3], we are content with the present compromise, and we scarcely ask ourselves how the dissecting-rooms are to be supplied when poverty has been abolished. No doubt there will always be enough men and women with such a religious devotion to science that they will volunteer for the dissecting-room in their wills. But our first instinct, if volunteers were called for, would be to shrink as if from a painful sacrifice.

I, for one, should find it difficult to bequeath my body into the

---

1 Bluebeard: 欧洲一种传说: 蓝须子杀了许多个妻子, 后来又娶了一个, 一天他出外去, 把锁钥交给妻子, 告诉她有一间房子千万不要开, 他走后, 他的妻子好奇心动了, 偏去开那房子, 里面有的却是前几位太太的尸首。她吓得心惊手战, 锁钥丢到地下, 沾了血迹。她用尽法子洗, 总洗不去。蓝须子回来看到钥匙上的血痕, 正要杀她, 她的兄弟刚好来看姊姊, 于是把这专会杀人的恶丈夫杀死了。

犯罪一样，笑他们，可是我们是多么不舒服地笑着。但是再过一千年人们或者会将这偷尸人同拐子当作科学功人，伯克同黑尔或者尊视做殉道者。我并不想人们将来会这样办，但是科学的进步或者是他们罪恶的结果。允许解剖室有时到坟地去找尸体同给它权利在那没有人领的养贫院穷人身体上用刀，是有同样坚固的理由。但是我们大部分人希望我们同我们朋友就在这生活昂贵的年头也不至于死在养贫院里，所以我们对现在这种妥协办法觉得满意，我们简直不去问当天下找不到穷人时候解剖室要由那里得来材料呢。当然天下有不少男女，对科学有这样宗教式的热心，在他们遗嘱里，他们自己献身给解剖室用。但是当征求这种甘心自荐的人们时候，我们头一个本能是退缩走开，像避一个苦痛的牺牲。

我就是一个不容易将我的身体赠送到医学生乱七八糟手里

---

2 Burke and Hare：英国有名偷尸首同拐人的两个犯人，后来都被绞死了。

3 workhouse：贫穷又无处依靠的人所居住的地方，每天照例做些工作，来换他们的衣食住的费用。

reckless hands of medical students. I do not know why, except that I cannot help somehow or other identifying my body with myself. Socrates was philosopher enough, on the eve of his death, to see his body as a shell and to say to himself: "That is not I." Most of us, however, though we might admit in our intelligences that our bodies were not we, would continue to think of them as ourselves in our imaginations. Whatever our essence, it is through the body that we have visited the earth, and we cannot dissociate from it any of the experiences that have made life so well worth living that we wish to go on with it[1]. One body was at least our inseparable consort, whether we went to church or to the tavern, whether we found our happiness in the sunny waist of the earth or by a coal fire at home, whether we played in the nursery or were kings of the football field, or fell in love or were rewarded with the great public prizes of the world. There has not been a single experience of our lives that would have been possible without hands, feet, heart, lungs, brain, mouth, eyes and ears. It is no wonder that St. Francis[2] on his death-bed, apologised to his body for having used it so ill, for without it there would have been no St. Francis, and the birds would have gone without their only sermon. How, then, can we be indifferent to such an associate?

---

1 to go on with it: to continue to live.
2 St. Francis: 他能够对鸟儿讲道，好比中国使顽石点头的生公。

的人。我不知道这是什么理由,除非是我免不了有些把我的躯体当做我整个的自己。苏格拉底到底是个真哲学家,能够在他死的前晚,把他身体看做个虚壳,对自己说,"那不是我。"可是我们多数人虽然在我们理智里可以承认我们的身体不就是我们,在想像中却总是继续把躯体算做就是自己。无论我们的本质是什么,我们是用这躯体来到地球上,一切使生命这样值得活,使我们希望再活下去的经验都不能和我们躯体分开。不管我们是到礼拜堂或者上酒馆,在大地向阳的山腰里或者家庭火炉旁得到的快乐,在育婴房游戏或者足球场上当王,在恋爱热狂里或者受世界上公众的大奖,我们的躯体最少是我们不可分的伴侣。我们一生里没有一个经验能不赖手,脚,心,肺,脑,口,眼,耳而实现。圣弗兰西斯在弥留时对他躯体道歉,因为待遇它太坏,这事是没有什么奇怪,因为没有躯体,圣弗兰西斯这人也不会存在了,鸟儿也失去了他们惟一的教谈,麻麻糊糊地死了。那么,我们对这样一个同伴,怎么能够不关心呢?

If a church made from the stones of the hills becomes sacred through associations, so that men, on entering it, take off their hats out of reverence for the temple of God, how much less surprising is it that a man should take thought for the fate of his body that is made of flesh and bones? Many men even leave instructions that honours shall be paid to their dead bodies such as they never demanded during life, like the Ulster Unionist[1] who asked that his body should be wrapped in a Union Jack and taken out and buried in Britannia's sea. Others have died the more easily because they knew that their remains (as the phrase goes) would be buried in some particular place—on the top of a hill, or in a cemetery with ghostly headstones visible from the sea at evening, or under the trees by an old church in a half-deserted village. I myself should feel melancholy if I thought I was to be buried in the Sahara or even in one of the colonies; and for a long time I should have felt a sharp pang if it had been foretold that I should be buried anywhere except in my own country; and I was particular even as to the exact spot in that. I do not know if I care so much as I once did. I fancy I have a growing objection to being buried anywhere at all. Nor do I take to the prospect of being burned. So long as one thinks of one's body as a living thing, one can hardly

---

1 Unionist：主张英国还是共爱尔兰合做一国，反对立法权分裂的人们。

若使山上石头盖的教堂由联带关系变做神圣东西，所以人们进去时候，因为对这上帝的庙宇表示尊敬，要脱下帽来，那么一个人对他那肉和骨做的躯体的运命会关心，这事更用不着奇怪了。好多人甚至于留下话来，要人们对他们死体有种礼遇，那是他们生时所没有要求过的，像亚鲁斯特地方一个主张联合主义者，他要大英联合帝国的国旗包着他的躯体，拿出投到不烈颠尼亚海里。有些人比较愿意死些，因为他们知道他们的遗体（话是这样说）会葬在一个特别地方——小山的顶上，或者在那墓地，那里鬼气阴森的墓碑黄昏时可以由海里看见或者在半荒弃的孤村里老教堂树下的一块地。若使我想起将来会埋在撒哈拉沙漠，或者就是埋在一个殖民地里，我自己会感到悲哀；设使有人对我预告，说我必定葬在异乡里，我会很久地觉到刺心的苦痛；甚至于在故乡那个地点长眠，我都要讲究。我不知道我现在有没有从前那么关心。我想我对于要葬在地下这回事，（不论是什么地方，）我反对的程度日日增加。火葬的结局，我也不爱。当我们看我们躯体还是个活东西时候，我们差不多想

imagine an end to it that does not seem almost as horrible as the dissecting-table. To be perpetuated as a mummy—who would care for that? Better to be cleansed swiftly by the earth into a skeleton in a Christian grave. When I had just left school and thought I was a pantheist[1], I used to take a sentimental pleasure, as other boys have done, in the prospect that flowers would spring from my tomb. I even liked the thought that I should help to fertilise the earth for those flowers. I cannot comfort myself so easily now, though I should be the happier if I thought the gardener would occasionally pay some small attention to my coverture. But I have really no taste for the underworld, and, if it were possible, I do not think I should ever visit it, but should continue on the floor of this excellent earth as long as the Wandering Jew[2]. It is said that in the end men grow tired of the body, and are glad enough to leave it. Those who do, I fancy, are bolder spirits than I. I am naturally a stay-at-home[3], and the only home in which I have lived all my life is my body. Born under Saturn[4], I have nevertheless been happy enough never to wish

---

1 pantheist：泛神论者（相信宇宙整个就是神，我们也是神的一部分，大地上一花一木都是神的表现）。

2 the Wandering Jew：犹太人侮辱了耶稣，耶稣就罚他们老在大地上东跑西走，没有片刻的休息，一直等到世界末日才止，这事耶稣做得实在不高明。

3 stay-at-home：home-keeping person 爱在家里住的人。

4 Saturn：参看60页"I bless my stars"注。

不出一个结局,而不是同解剖桌一样地可怕。把尸体老是保存着,做个木乃伊——谁愿意这样子呢?在基督教徒的墓里快快地给土洗净成个骷髅倒还好些。我刚离学校,想自己是个泛神主义者时节,我像别的小孩所干过一样,我想起将来好花会由我坟里生出,我有一种痴心的欣欢。我甚至于爱想为这花,我要化作养料去把土弄肥沃。我现在不能这么容易来安慰自己,虽然若使我想起那花匠有时对我这永久的盖被会费点心,我心里还是会高兴些。可是真的,我对地下世界并无爱好,倘然是办得到,我想我永不会自己到那里去,只是在这乐土的地板上继续地滞留着,滞得同"游荡无所归的犹太人"一样久。据说人老了对这躯体生了厌倦,很愿意离开去。我想有这种心境的人的精神是比我勇敢。我生性是爱在家里住着,我一生无时不住在里面的惟一的家是我的躯体。虽然命带土星,我却都还快乐,不想将我的躯体去换一个更好的。若使我愿意做个更好人,

to change it for a better. If I have wished to be a better man, I have still wishes for the new spirit to inhabit the same body, for, though it is a body that no man could be proud of, not being built in any of the noble styles of architecture, I am used to it and am bound to it by all manner of sympathies[1]. Not that I have looked after it as well as I might have done. I have allowed it to sink into dilapidation and disrepair, so that it already resembles more than it should a piece of antiquity[2]. But even the crooked man with the crooked cat probably lived happily enough in his crooked little house, and would not have left it without compulsion. Hence, though I cannot share their faith, I should not be sorry to think that those Christians were right who believe that on the last day the body will be whisked through the air to become the house of the soul again in a better world. I do not defend myself or pretend that this is a laudable attitude. I admire Socrates, indeed, and all those who have despised the body as a fragile pot or as grass that withers, but I cannot help recognising the fact that I am not of their company.

On the other hand, I cannot go so far as those people who shrink from the grave all the more because they cannot endure the thought of the rain beating down upon them by night and chilling

---

1 all manner of sympathy: every kind of sympathy.
2 it already resembles more than it should a piece of antiquity：这是英国一首儿歌中的话。

我还是希望新灵魂在这旧躯体里住，因为虽然我这个躯体并没有照什么建筑的高贵格式做的，没有人会把它拿来自夸，我对这躯体却很惯了，有各种的同情把我同它捆起。我对它的看护却没有尽我的能力。我让这躯体沉到破毁倾颓的状态，所以我身体已经未老先衰了。但是一个弯背的人，有个弯身的猫子，或者在那弯颓的小屋里住得很快乐，不是受强迫，还不愿意离开那屋子。所以若使相信末日到时躯体会飞过空中，再做在更好世界灵魂的房子的基督教徒是对的，虽然我不能够同他们有同样的信仰，我也是很高兴。我并不替自己辩护，或者妄说这是个可赞美的态度。真的，我羡慕苏格拉底同一切看轻躯体，只当做是一个脆弱的瓶子或者会枯的草的人们，但是我不得不承认我不是他们的俦侣。

有些人因为想起雨点在夜里打到他们，冷了他们无知觉的骨头，心里难过，所以更退缩怕到坟墓去，这种人我却也难同他们合伙。最近在某一本书上，我念到一件故事，说当他所爱

their senseless bones. I read somewhere lately that, when the woman he loved died, Abraham Lincoln was almost driven mad during a storm by the feeling that the wind was howling and the rain falling on her grave. Others have told me that they share this feeling, and I know a man who said that he would hate to be buried in a certain graveyard because it was "very damp." But then he was subject to rheumatism[1]. His objection was as valid, however, as is the objection of most of us to lie, misshapen and skinny, under the eyes of a professor on the dissecting-table. We impute to our dead bodies many of the senses and shames of the living, and we shudder without reason at the thought of things occurring to them that could injure us only while we are alive. Thus do we give ourselves an extension of life in our fancies. It seems as though we must be surer that life is worth living than that death is worth dying. But, even on this matter, there is room for hope.

---

1 rheumatism：痛风症多半由潮湿得来，这位先生怕他死后又会患这病，所以不愿意葬在潮湿地方。

的女人死后，林肯在个风雨夜差不多疯狂了，为的想起这时候风正怒号着雨正狂打着在她墓上面。别人告诉我他们也有这类感觉，我认得一个人，他说他不愿意埋在一个坟地里，因为那里土"很潮湿"。但是那时他正患风湿症。然而他这个反对同我们大多数不愿躯体不全有皮无肉地放在解剖桌上教授眼前有同样坚固的理由。我们将好多生人的羞耻心同感觉放在我们死体上，我们想到死体受那只在我们生时才能损害我们的事情时，我们没有理由地战栗。这样在想像中我们给自己一种生命的延长。我们好像对活值得活比死值得死应当更有把握些。但是就是在死这回事，我们还存有希望的余地。

Sir Walter Raleigh

(1861—1922)

Don Quixote[1]

A Spanish knight, about fifty years of age, who lived in great poverty in a village of La Mancha, gave himself up[2] so entirely to reading the romances of chivalry, of which he had a large collection, that in the end they turned his brain[3], and nothing would satisfy him but that he must ride abroad on his old horse, armed with spear and helmet, a knight-errant, to encounter all adventures, and to redress the innumerable wrongs of the world. He induced a neighbour of his, a poor and ignorant peasant called Sancho Panza, mounted on a

---

1 Don Quixote: 林琴南先生译过, 书名译做《魔侠传》。关于这部书周作人先生有几篇很有趣味的文章, 散见《自己的园地》同《语丝》。在中国小说里, 要找出和吉河德先生相像的人物, 很不容易。我想了三天三夜, 才想出《儒林外史》里风流儒雅的杜少卿, 这篇里许多批评这位仗矛飞马奔走风尘的骑士的话都可以用在河房里啸遨湖山的贤公子身上, 可惜

吉诃德先生

　　一个西班牙的武士，大约五十岁年纪，在拉曼差村中度着非常穷苦的生活，拚命地念那谈游侠的浪漫小说，这种书他收集了好多，最后竟把他头脑弄糊涂了，没有事情能满足他，一心想要骑了他那老马到外面去，提着长矛，戴起甲胄，当一个游侠，去冒一切的危险，来伸雪世界上数不尽的不平事件。他引诱了一个邻居，一个又穷又傻的农夫，名字叫做山差·邦札，

王胡子实在比不上山差·邦札，吴敬梓先生到底逊西班牙文士 Miguel de Cervantes Saavedra（1547—1616）一筹。
　　2　gave himself up: addicted himself to.
　　3　turned his brain: made him mad.

very good ass, to accompany him as squire. The knight saw the world in the mirror of his beloved romances; he mistook inns for enchanted castles, windmills for giants, and country wenches for exiled princesses. His high spirit[1] and his courage never failed him, but his illusions led him into endless trouble. In the name of justice and chivalry[2] he intruded himself on all whom he met, and assaulted all whom he took to be making an oppressive or discourteous use of power. He and his poor squire were beaten, trounced, cheated, and ridiculed on all hands[3], until in the end, by the kindliness of his old friends in the village, and with the help of some new friends who had been touched[4] by the amiable and generous character of his illusions, the knight was cured of his whimsies and was led back to his home in the village, there to die.

That is the story of Don Quixote: it seems a slight framework for what, without much extravagance, may be called the wisest and most splendid book in the world. It is an old man's book; there is in it all the wisdom of a fiery heart that has learned patience. Shakespeare and Cervantes died on the same day, but if Cervantes had died at the same age as Shakespeare we should have had no *Don Quixote*. Shakespeare himself has written nothing so full of the

---

1 high spirit: lofty spirit.
2 in the name of justice and chivalry: as representing justice and chivalry 代表公理同武士的精神。

骑一匹很好的驴子,跟他当从卒去。这个武士只有从他所爱的浪漫小说这面镜子里看到世界;他把小旅馆错当做魔堡,风车错当做巨人,又把乡村姑娘错当做流落在外面的公主。他的豪气同勇敢始终不衰,但是他的幻觉却给了无穷的麻烦给他。用保障公道同游侠精神的名义,他把自己插入在他所碰到的人们里面,凡是他以为是拿权力来做压迫或者横暴用的人们,他都要殴打他们。他同那可怜的从卒到处挨打,受鞭挞,被骗,受人们的嘲笑,等到最后靠着他村里老朋友的好意,同那些被他幻觉所含有的可爱而慷慨的性质所感动了的几个新朋友的帮助,这武士才医好了他的瞎想,给人带回到他故乡家里,以后就死在那里。

　　这是《吉诃德先生》这本书的本事:这好像是一个琐屑的骨子,在可以叫做世界上最聪明,最伟大的书面上讲起来,没有什么虚说。这是一本老年人做的书,里面包含着已经懂得忍耐的热烈心的一切智慧。莎士比亚同塞文狄斯是同日死的,但是若使塞文狄斯的命也只有莎士比亚那么长,我们就不会有《吉诃德先生》这本书。莎士比亚自己没有写过什么东西,有这

---

3 on all hands: from every one.
4 touched: moved into sympathy.

diverse stuff of experience, so quietly and steadily illuminated by gentle wisdom, so open-eyed in discerning the strength of the world; and Shakespeare himself is not more courageous in championing the rights of the gallant heart. Suppose the Governor of Barataria[1] had been called on to decide the cause between these two great authors. His judgments were often wonderfully simple and obvious. Perhaps he would have ruled that whereas Shakespeare died at the age of fifty-two and Cervantes lived seventeen years longer, a man shall give his days and nights to the study[2] of Shakespeare until he is older than ever Shakespeare was, and then, for the solace of his later years, shall pass on[3] to the graver school of Cervantes. Not every man lives longer than Shakespeare; and, of those who do, not every man masters the art and craft of growing older with the passage of years, so that, by this rule, the Spanish gentleman would have a much smaller circle of intimates than the High Bailiff's[4] son of Stratford. And so he has; yet his world-wide popularity is none the less assured. He has always attracted, and will always attract, a great company of readers who take a simple and legitimate[5] delight in the comic distresses of the deluded Don, in the tricks upon him, in the

---

1 the Governor of Barataria: 《吉诃德先生》书里一个人物。
2 give his days and nights to the study: study diligently.
3 pass on: proceed.
4 the High Bailiff's: 莎翁的父亲是做Stratford地方的高等典吏。

样充满了经验的各色材料,这样恬静稳健地照出温和的智慧,对于世界的力量有这么明亮地看到;就是替雄豪心肠人辩护说话时候,莎士比亚也不能比他勇敢。设使请把拉替力亚的地方官来裁判这两位大作家的案件。他的判决辞常是简单明白得出奇。或者他要规定,因为莎士比亚是五十二岁死的,塞文狄斯比他多活十七年,一个人所以要整天整夜念莎士比亚,等他活到比莎士比亚死的时候年岁还大,以后,做他暮年的安慰,他可以到塞文狄斯所开的更严肃的学校去。然而不是每个人都能够比莎士比亚命长,而且有那么长寿命的人里,不是每个人都学到随着年岁长进的法术,所以照这个规定,这位西班牙先生的熟朋友一定比不上那斯徒拉福高等典吏儿子的范围那么广。他确是没有那么多好朋友;但是他那得天下人的欢迎的力还是一样地不会失丢。他老是,将来还是一样地,摄引一大群读者,当这班读者看到这位糊涂的武士先生所受的可笑苦难,人家同他捣乱的诡计,他那种多愁多难的古怪外表,他所听见的情史

---

5 legitimate:proper 人们对于旁人很滑稽地受苦,一定会觉得好笑,这是自然而然的,并不是出于残忍,所以说是 legitimate(合理的,合法的)。

woful absurdity of his appearance, in the many love-stories and love-songs that he hears, in the variety of the characters that he meets, in the wealth of the incidents and events that spring up, a joyous crop, wherever he sets his foot, and not least, perhaps, in the beatings, poundings, scratchings, and tumblings in the mire that are his daily portion. That is to say, those who care little or nothing for Don Quixote may yet take pleasure in the life[1] that is in his book; and his book is full of life.

We have no very ample record of the life experiences of Cervantes, which are distilled in this, his greatest book. We know that he was a soldier, and fought against the Turks at Lepanto, where his left hand was maimed for life; that he was made prisoner some years later by the Moors, and suffered five years' captivity at Algiers; that he attempted with others to escape, and when discovered and cross-examined took the whole responsibility on himself; that at last he was ransomed by the efforts of his family and friends, and returned to Spain, there to live as best he could the life of a poor man of letters, with intermittent Government employ, for thirty-six more years. He wrote sonnets and plays, pawned his family's goods, and was well acquainted with the inside of prisons. He published the First Part of *Don Quixote* in 1605—that is to say, in his fifty-eighth year—and thenceforward enjoyed a high reputation, though his poetry continued.

---

1 the life：指书中充满了有趣的事情，奇怪的脚色，到处都是非常热闹。

恋歌，他所碰到的各样各色人物，他每到一个地方立刻生出来的许多灾祸事故（一大堆有趣的事情），他们得到一种简单纯粹的快乐，或者他们同样高兴地读到他的挨打，受捶，脸孔给人家抓破，同在泥洼里打转，这些他天天尝着的事情。这就是说，不大注意或者毫不留心吉诃德先生本身的人们也可以由那书里的活泼热闹情境得到趣味；他的书却是充满了这活泼热闹的情境。

我们对塞文狄斯自己一生的经验没有什么充分的记载，他的经验是结晶在这本书里，他最伟大的著作。我们知道他是个军人，在拉朋吐地方同土耳人打仗，他的左手受伤变成了残疾；过几年他又给摩尔人监禁起来，在亚鲁格尔斯受了五年的囚奴生活；他同旁人合伙想法逃走，被人发觉，当受审问时候，他将全部责任推到自己身上；最后藉他家族同朋友的力量赎回来，回到西班牙去，在那里勉强地过一个穷文人的生活，有时干些政府给他的差事，就这么样子再活了三十六年。他做过十四行诗同戏剧，把他家里东西拿去上当铺过，还很知道监狱的内容。在一六零五——就是说，在他五十六〔八〕岁时候——他出版第一部的《吉诃德先生》，从此以后享了盛名，虽然他的穷困还是继续着。

In 1615 the Second Part of *Don Quixote* appeared, wherein the author makes delightful play with the First Part by treating it as a book well known to all the characters of the story. In the following year he died, clothed in the Franciscan habit, and was buried in the convent of the Barefooted Trinitarian Nuns in Madrid. No stone marks his grave, but his spirit still wanders the world in the person of the finest gentleman of all the realms of fact and fable[1], who still maintains in discourse with all whom he meets that the thing of which the world has most need is knights-errant, to do honour to women, to fight for the cause of the oppressed, and to right the wrong.[2] "This, then, gentlemen", he may still be heard saying, "it is to be a knight-errant, and what I have spoken of is the order of chivalry, in the which, as I have already said, I, though a sinner, have made profession; the same which these famous knights profess do I profess; and that is why I am travelling through these deserts and solitary places, in quest of adventures, with deliberate resolve to offer my arm and my person to the most dangerous adventure which fortune may present, in aid of the weak and needy." And the world is still incredulous and dazed. "By these words which he uttered", says the author in brief comment on the foregoing speech, "the travellers were quite convinced that Don Quixote was out of his wits".

---

1 the finest gentleman of all the realms of fact and fable：指吉诃德先生。

在一六一五，第二部的《吉诃德先生》出版，在这部书里作者很有趣味地将他那第一部书拿来开玩笑，把他当作是这故事里面的人物全都知道的一本书。第二年他死了，穿个佛兰西斯教徒的衣服，埋在马德力的一个"三位一体派跣足尼姑庵"里。没有碑石指出他的墓，但他的精神已化做了一个现实同理想两境界里最温文秀雅的君子，在世界上逍遥着，碰着人谈论时，他还是主张世界上最需要的东西是游侠，去尊敬妇女，替被压迫的人们争斗，代天下人打不平。"先生们"，我们还可以听到他说，"这就是当游侠，我所谈的就是武士派，我已经告诉你们过，我虽然不是完人，我却拿这个做我的专业，干这班有名侠士所干的事情；所以我要旅行这些荒野同寂寞地方，去冒各种危险，我曾考虑过，下个决心，为着要扶弱济贫，我愿将我这手臂同身体贡献给命运呈现在我面前的最大危险"。世界是仍然多惑而且杂乱。"由他们所说的几句话看来"，作者对前面那篇话加个按语说，"旅客们完全相信吉诃德先生有神经病了"。

塞文狄斯虽然死了，他的精神却包含在吉诃德先生性格里，天天与读者会晤。

   2 to do honour to women, to fight for the cause of the oppressed, and to right the wrong：这三样事是骑士的天职。

It has often been said, and is still sometimes repeated by good students of Cervantes[1], that his main object in writing *Don Quixote* was to put an end to the influence of the romances of chivalry. It is true that these romances were the fashionable reading of his age, that many of them were trash, and that some of them were pernicious trash. It is true also that the very scheme of his book lends itself to a scathing[2] exposure of their weaknesses, and that the moral[3] is pointed in the scene of the inquisition of the books, where the priest, the barber, the housekeeper, and the niece destroy the greater part of his library by fire. But how came it that Cervantes knew the romances so well, and dwelt on some of their incidents in such loving detail[4]? Moreover, it is worth nothing that not a few of them are excluded by name from the general condemnation. *Amadis of Gaul* is spared, because it is "the best of all books of the kind". Equal praise is given to *Palmerin of England*; while of *Tirante the White* the priest himself declares that it is a treasure of delight and a mine of pastime.

"Truly, I declare to you, gossip, that in its style this is the best book in the world. Here the knights eat and sleep, and die in their beds, and make their wills before they die, with other things in which the rest of the books of this kind are wanting."

---

1 good students of Cervantes: good scholars who make a study of Cervantes.
2 scathing: injuring.
3 the moral: the meaning of the book.

有句常说的话，好多研究塞文狄斯的人有时也提到，就是说他写《吉诃德先生》的大目的是要消灭武士浪漫小说的影响。真的，他那时候时髦的读品是这些浪漫小说，里面好多是没有价值，有许多是有害的没有价值的东西。这也是真的，就是《吉诃德先生》这部书的布局也把这类小说的弱点痛快淋漓地暴露出来，他这本书的真意可以在检查书籍那件事情里看出，那回牧师，理发匠，管家人，同甥女把他所藏的浪漫小说大部分用火烧去。但塞文狄斯怎样会这么清楚地知道这些浪漫小说，说到它们里面的事情时又是津津有味，详详细细呢？而且，好几本没有受这次普通火葬的，他特别提出名字来，这也是值得注意的事。《高鲁的亚马的斯》留着，"因为这在那类书里算是最好的。"《英吉利的帕鲁买林》也得同样地赞美；牧师自己都说《白贮能提》是快乐的宝库，消遣的富源。

"真的，我要告诉你，教母，论这本书的文体，这是世界上最好的书，在这本书里武士们也有吃东西，睡觉，死在床上，死以前也做好他的遗嘱，还有旁的事情，都是这类书别本所没有的。"

---

4 loving detail：因为爱那些书，所以说得详详细细，津津有味。

But even stronger evidence of the esteem that Cervantes felt for the best of the romances is to be found in his habit of linking their names with the poems of Homer and Virgil. So, in the course of instruction given by Don Quixote to Sancho Panza, while they dwelt in the wilds of the Sierra, Morena, Ulysses[1] is cited as the model of prudence and patience, Aeneas[2] as the greatest of pious sons and expert captains, and Amadis as the "pole star, the morning star, the sun of valiant and enamoured knights, whom all we have to copy, who do battle under the banner of love and chivalry. " It would indeed be a strange thing if a book which is so brave an exercise of the creative imagination were mainly destructive in its aim, and deserved no higher honour than a scavenger. The truth is that the book is so many-sided that all kinds of tastes and beliefs can find their warrant[3] in it. The soul of it[4] is an irony so profound that but few of its readers have explored it to the depth. It is like a mine, deep below deep; and much good treasure is to be found at the more easily accessible levels. All irony criticises the imperfect ideas and theories of mankind, not by substituting for them other ideas and other theories, less imperfect, but by placing the facts of life, in mute comment[5],

---

1 Ulysses: Homer 所做史诗里的英雄。
2 Aeneas: Virgil 所做史诗里的英雄。
3 can find their warrant: can find their ground.

但是塞文狄斯对最好的浪漫小说的敬重,我们可以由他常将它们的书名同荷马和维即鲁的诗连在一块提起这点上更显明地看出。所以当他们住在石于拉穆冷拉旷野,吉河德先生教导山差·邦札时候,他提出优尼谢斯做谨慎同耐心的模范,意尼斯算做最大的孝子能将,亚马的斯却真做"被一位贵女迷住了的勇敢武士们的北极星,启明星同太阳,这班武士在爱情同游侠的旗帜下打仗,都是我们的好榜样"。若使一部这么大胆,想像崭新的著作,大部分目的却在破坏方面,那真是一件奇事,而这本书也只像个清道夫,不能得我们什么大敬礼。实在因为这本书的方面极多,一切趣味信仰都能由里面抓到一个根据。这书的真髓是一种讥讽,但是太深了,只有几个读者能够看透。好像一个矿,深处下面还有深处;许多好宝贝在容易走到的那层也可以得到。一切讥讽来批评人类不对的意思同理论时,不是用一种另外更不对的意思同理论来代替,只是将事实放在那

---

4 the soul of it: the real meaning or spirit of it 真正精神。

5 in mute comment: 不要讲出,任何人一看都能明白的论调。

alongside of the theories. The Ruler of the World¹ is the great master of irony; and man has been permitted to share some part of his enjoyment in the purifying power of fact². The weaker and more querulous members of the race commonly try to enlist³ the facts in the service of their pet ideas. A grave and deep spirit like Cervantes knows that the facts will endure no such servitude. They will not take orders from those who call for⁴ their verdict, nor will they be content to speak only when they are asked to speak. They intrude suddenly, in the most amazing and irrelevant fashion, on the carefully ordered plans of humanity. They cannot be explained away⁵, and many a man who thought to have guarded himself against surprise has been surprised by love and death⁶.

Every one sees the irony of *Don Quixote* in its first degree, and enjoys it in its more obvious forms. This absurd old gentleman, who tries to put his antiquated ideas into action in a busy, selfish, prosy⁷

1　the Ruler of the World: the God.
2　the purifying power of fact：各种乱七八糟的意见学说，把人们弄得糊涂了，事实一来立刻可以拨云雾而见天日，所以说有 purifying power。
3　to enlist: to get the support of.
4　call for: demand.
5　explained away: softened down.
6　has been surprised by love and death："爱"和"死"是小品文家最喜欢讨论的题材，尤其是"死"，因为死这题目可以容纳无限幻想，最合于捧着烟斗靠在躺椅时的沉思默虑。Bacon, Montaigne, Addison, Steele,

理论旁边，做个没有说出，看者自知的评语。"宇宙之王"是个讥讽大家；人类也可以分得些他这种用事实洗净理论的快乐。比较孱弱好争的人们常常要事实来帮他那无聊的理论的忙。像塞文狄斯这样一个严肃精深的人知道事实是不能忍受这种奴使。它们不肯由那要它们下个判断的人那里得到命令，它们也不愿只在人家要它们说话时节说话。它们常常非常惊人，毫不相干地忽然冲进那人们细心料理得很好的计划里。它们不是解释得丢的，好多人自己以为很有把握不会受惊，却给爱情同死亡吓住了。

《吉诃德先生》书里最浅的那层讥讽，谁也看得到，谁对这容易了解的讥讽，也感到趣味。这位糊涂老先生想把他那老旧的思想在这忙碌自私平庸粗俗的世界上应用，就是由智识能力

Leigh Hunt, De Quincey, Smith, Belloc 等都有很好的关于"死"的作品。Stevenson，一个句斟字酌的近代小品文家，在他的小品集《贻青年少女》(*Virginibus Puerisque*) 开头四篇里讨论结婚和爱情。凡是对于结婚顾虑到将来的幸福而不愿轻率从事的人们，最好把这四篇文章仔细玩味一下，无论如何，总可得到不少的启示和帮助。Stevenson 也说过："There is only one event in life which really astonishes a man and startles him out of his prepared opinions."

7 prosy: insipid.

world, is a figure of fun even to the meanest intelligence. But, with more thought, there comes a check to our frivolity. Is not all virtue and all goodness in the same case as Don Quixote? Does the author, after all, mean to say that the world is right, and that those who try to better¹ it are wrong? If that is what he means, how is it that at every step of our journey² we come to like the Don better, until in the end we can hardly put a limit to our love and reverence for him? Is it possible that the criticism is double-edged³, and that what we are celebrating with our laughter is the failure of the world?

A wonderful thing in Cervantes's handling of his story is his absolute honesty and candour. He does not mince matters⁴. His world behaves as the world may be expected to behave when its daily interests are violently disordered by a lunatic. Failure upon failure dogs⁵ the steps of poor Don Quixote, and he has no popularity to redeem his material disasters. "He who writes of me", says the Don pensively, in his discussion with the bachelor Sampson, "will please very few"; and the only comfort the bachelor can find for him is that

---

1 to better: to improve.

2 at every step of our journey: 把读书比做旅行，一章一章地看下去，好像是一山一水地领略风光。近代批评家 Anatole France 把批评当作心灵的探险；若把这学说应用到这句上，那又多一层深刻的意思了。

3 double-edged: 两面俱利的刀。（此处指一方面我们笑吉诃德先生的受骗，一方面笑世俗的卑鄙。）

最下等人看来，也觉得是一个可笑的人物。但是，再想一下，我们的轻浮乱笑就会有一个制止了。天下所有的道德好心是不是都同吉诃德先生在同样的情形中呢？作者到底是不是要说，世界已经很好了，所以这班想去把它再变好的人们是错的？若使这是他的意思，为什么在我们念这书时节，我们一步一步地觉得这位武士先生更可爱，等到最后我们对他的爱敬简直是无限量的？书中所含的批评会不会像个两边都是锋利的刀，而我们看着很高兴地狂笑的事情会不会就是世界上的缺陷呢？

塞文狄斯写这部小说时的一件奇事是他那绝对忠实同坦白的态度。他并没有什么事情说得半吞半吐。他书里的世界的一切动作是像一个日常事情给个疯子捣乱得乱七八糟的世界。失败接连着失败跟在这可怜的吉诃德先生脚后，他当时又没有什么赫赫虚名可以补偿他这物质上的灾祸。"凡是把我这个人拿来写成一本书的人"，这位武士先生当他同单身汉森卜新谈论时候，他沉思地说，"只能使极少数人高兴"；这位单身汉替他找

---

4 does not mince matters: does speak bluntly.

5 dogs（v.t.）: never ceases to follow.

the number of fools is infinite, and that the First Part of his adventures has delighted them all. As an example of Cervantes's treatment take one of the earliest of these adventures, the rescue of the boy Andres from the hands of his oppressor. As he rode away from the inn, on the first day of his knighthood, while yet he was unfurnished with a squire, Don Quixote heard cries of complaint from a thicket near by. He thanked Heaven for giving him so early an opportunity of service, and turned his horse aside to where he found a farmer beating a boy. Don Quixote, with all knightly formality, called the farmer a coward[1], and challenged him to single combat. The farmer, terrified by the strange apparition, explained that the boy was his servant and by gross carelessness had lost sheep for him at the rate of one a day. The matter was at last settled by the farmer liberating the boy and promising to pay him in full his arrears of wages; whereupon the knight rode away, well pleased. Then the farmer tied up the boy again, and beat him more severely than ever, till at the last he loosed him, and told him to go and seek redress from his champion. "So the boy departed sobbing, and his master stayed behind laughing; and after this manner did the valorous Don Quixote right that wrong." Later on, when the knight and his squire are in the wilds, with the

---

1 called the farmer a coward: 按骑士习惯，必先受人侮辱然后才比武，所以吉诃德先生故意骂农夫一句，给农夫一种比武的藉口。

出的唯一的安慰只有这点，就是天下愚人的数目是无限的，他们却都喜欢他冒险故事的第一部。做一个例来说明塞文狄斯写小说的方法，让我把一个这武士最初的冒险故事拿来述一遍，就是那回将小孩安特烈斯由压迫者手里救出的事情。当吉诃德先生成了武士的第一天，那时他还没有一个从卒，他骑马离开了小旅馆时，吉诃德先生听到邻近丛林里有悲诉的呼声。他谢谢上天这么早就给他一个履行他职务的机会，把马转到那里去，在那里他看到一个农夫打着一个小孩。吉诃德先生用了武士那一套礼节，将那农夫叫做懦夫，挑战他来两人对打。农夫看到出现了这样一个罕见的怪物，心里害怕，就解释说这小孩是他的仆人，粗心得很，每天总要丢了一只羊。这事最后解决的法子是农夫恢复小孩的自由，答应还给小孩他所欠的工钱；这位武士心里很高兴地骑马走了。农夫就将小孩重新捆起，比平常更利害地打他一顿，最后才松开绳子，叫他去找他的保护者再来伸雪。"因此这小孩哭着走开，他的主人站在后面大笑；勇敢的吉诃德先生是这样子替人抱不平的。"后来当这武士同从卒在

company whom chance has gathered around them, the boy appears again, and Don Quixote narrates the story of his deliverance as an illustration of the benefits conferred on the world by knight-errantry.

"All that your worship[1] says is true," replies the lad, "but the end of the business was very much the contrary of what your worship imagines." "How contrary?" said Don Quixote. "Did he not pay thee, then?" "He not only did not pay me," said the boy, "but as soon as your worship had got outside the wood, and we were alone, he tied me again to the same tree, and gave me so many lashes that he left me flayed like St. Bartholomew[2]; and at every lash he uttered some jest or scoff, to make a mock of your worship; and if I had not felt so much pain, I would have laughed at what he said... For all this your worship is to blame[3], because if you had held on[4] your way, and had not meddled with other people's business, my master would have been content to give me a dozen or two lashes, and afterwards he would have released me and paid me what he owed. But as your worship insulted him and called him bad names, his anger was kindled; and as he could not avenge himself on you, he let fly[5] the tempest on me."

---

1 your worship: 一种尊称。
2 St. Bartholomew: 是被人剥皮弄死的。
3 is to blame: deserves blame.

旷野时候，刚好那里偶然有一群人，那个小孩也在内，吉诃德先生就述他关于救人的故事，做游侠给世界以利益的一个例子。

"您老爷所说的，全是真的"，那小孩子答应，"但是事情的结局同你老爷所想的大大相反。""怎么相反？"吉诃德先生说。"以后他没有还你的钱吗？""他不但没有还我钱"，那小孩说，"而且你老爷一走出森林，只剩我同他两个人的时候，他重新把我缚在起先那个树上，鞭打我那么利害，使我简直变做同圣巴所落苗一样地剥去一层皮；每打一下，他就说几句滑稽或者轻蔑的话，来嘲笑你老爷；若使我不是受那么多苦痛，我对他所说的话简直会笑起来……这么多事情全是你老爷弄起来的，因为若使你走你的路，不管旁人的事，我主人打我一二十下，也就会打够，以后他会把我解下，还我他所欠的钱。但是因为你老爷侮辱了他，骂了他好多话，把他的怒气激起来了；他因为不能在你身上报仇，就把他全部的雷霆发在我身上了。"

4　held on: parsued.

5　let fly: discharged.

Don Quixote sadly admits his error, and confesses that he ought to have remembered that "no churl keeps the word he gives if he finds that it does not suit him to keep it." But he promises Andres that he will yet see him righted; and with that the boy's terror awakes. "For the love of God, Sir knight-errant," he says, "if you meet me again, and see me, being cut to pieces, do not rescue me, nor help me, but leave me to my pain; for, however great it be, it cannot be greater than will come to me from the help of your worship—whom, with all the knights-errant ever born into the world, may God confound!" With that he ran away, and Don Quixote stood very much abashed by his story, so that the rest of the company had to take great care that they did not laugh outright and put him to confusion.

At no point in the story does Cervantes permit the reader to forget that the righter of wrongs must not look in this world for either success or praise. The indignities heaped upon that gentle and heroic soul almost revolt[1] the reader, as Charles Lamb remarked. He is beaten and kicked; he has his teeth knocked out, and consoles himself with the thought that these hardships are incident to his profession; his face is all bedaubed with mud, and he answers with grave politeness to the mocks of those who deride him. When he stands sentry on the back of his horse at the inn, to guard the sleepers,

---

1 revolt: affect with disgust.

吉诃德先生悲哀地认了错，自己说他应当记着"没有坏人会践言的，若使他觉得不大方便照他所答应的话干。"但是他允许安特烈斯，说要替他报复；听这话，小孩又害怕起来了。"为上帝的爱起见，游侠老爷"，他说，"若使你再碰着我，看我给人砍做碎块，请你也不要救我，也不要帮助我，还是让我挨苦痛好；因为无论多大苦痛，总不及由你老爷帮助我以后，我所受苦痛那么大——我愿上帝使你同一切生在世上的游侠都倒了霉！"说着他就跑开了，吉诃德先生听这故事自己觉得很惭愧，所以其余人要很小心没有笑出来，免得使他难堪。

书里没有一处地方，塞文狄斯使读者忘记了这样的事，就是说，替人打不平的人在这世界上绝不要希望得到什么成功同赞美。真像查理斯·兰姆所说，这个文雅英武的好汉所受的一大堆侮辱差不多使读者看得都不高兴。他挨打，被踢，牙齿也遭打落，只好自己安慰，心里想这些苦痛都是干这种事业的人所常受的；他脸上被人满满地涂上泥，他很严肃地答应那愚弄他的人们的嘲笑。当他在旅馆里骑在马背上做哨兵来保护那些睡眠者的时候，管马厩的一个女仆马力多尼斯，把他的手伸到

the stable wench, Maritornes, gets him to reach up his hand to an upper window, or rather a round hole in the wall of the hayloft, whereupon she slips a running noose over his wrist and ties the rope firmly to a bar within the loft. In this posture, and in continual danger of being hung by the arm if his horse should move away, he stands till dawn, when four travellers knock at the gate of the inn. He at once challenges them for their discourtesy in disturbing the slumbers of those whom he is guarding. Even the Duke and the Duchess, who feel kindly to Don Quixote and take him under their care, are quite ready to play rough practical jokes[1] on him. It is while he is their guest that his face is all seratched and clawed by frightened cats turned loose in his bedroom at night. His friends in the village were kinder than this, but they, to get him home, carried him through the country in a latticed cage on poles, like a wild beast, for the admiration of the populace; and he bethought himself, "As I am a new knight in the world, and the first that hath revived the forgotten exercise of chivalry, these are newly invented forms of enchantment." His spirit rises superior to all his misfortunes, and his mind remains as serene as a cloudless sky.

But Don Quixote, it may be objected, is mad. Here the irony of Cervantes finds a deeper level. Don Quixote is a high-minded idealist,

---

1 practical jokes: tricks played on a person 口说的笑话，居然拿来实行，自然是恶作剧了。

上层窗口，或者也可以说是草棚的围墙上一个圆洞，在那里她将一个活结滑到他的手腕节，那绳子就坚固地结在草架里面的一个杠子上。若使他的马走开，他就有一个手吊着的危险，在这样情形中，他一直站到天亮，那时有四个旅客在客栈门口打门。他立刻向他们挑战，因为他们这样打扰他所保护的睡觉者实在是个无礼行为。就是和他很有感情，照顾他的公爵同公爵夫人也很愿意同他开些粗野的玩笑。这是当他做他们的客人时候，他脸孔给故意赶到他房里的一群惊慌的猫全抓破了。村里的朋友对待他还好些，但是他们带他回家时，用杠子抬个有格子的笼，将他像个野兽放在里面，给群众观赏；他自己想，"因为我是世界上一个新武士，是头一个将这已经忘了的游侠举动恢复起来，这或者是一种新发明的用魔力囚闭人的法子"。他的精神总是超在一切患难之上，他的心始终是像云净天空一样地晴明安静。

但是人们可以反对说吉诃德先生是疯了。这里塞文狄斯的讥讽是更深了一层。吉诃德先生是个心境高超的理想主义者，

who sees all things by the light of his own lofty preconceptions. To him every woman is beautiful and adorable; everything that is said to him is worthy to be heard with attention and respect; every community of men, even the casual assemblage of lodgers at an inn, is a society founded on strict rules of mutual consideration and esteem. He shapes his behaviour in accordance with these ideas, and is laughed at for his pains. But he has a squire, Sancho Panza, who is a realist[1] and loves food and sleep, who sees the world as it is, by the light of common day. Sancho, it might be supposed, is sane, and supplies a sure standard whereby to measure his master's deviation from the normal. Not at all; Sancho, in his own way, is as mad as his master. If the one is betrayed by fantasy, the other is betrayed, with as ludicrous a result, by common sense. The thing is well seen in the question of the island, the government of which is to be entrusted to Sancho when Don Quixote comes into his kingdom. Sancho, though he would have seen through the pretences of any merely corrupt bargainer, recognises at once that his master is disinterested and truthful, and he believes all he hears about the island. He spends much thought on the scheme, and passes many criticisms on it. Sometimes he protests that he is quite unfit for the position of a governor, and that his wife would cut a poor figure[2] as a governor's lady. At other

---

1 a realist: 实体论者（和理想主义者相对，指那班计较利害的人）。

他用他自己的先见来照看一切东西。由他看起来，每个女人都是美丽可钦的；无论对他说的什么话都值得很注意很尊重听着；每群人就是随便在客店聚集的客人们，都是根据了互相关心同看重的严格原则而成立的社会。他的行为是由这些意思脱胎出来的，所以人们笑他挨了许多苦，但是他有一个从卒山差·邦札，这从卒却是个实际主义者，爱吃贪睡，用常识来看世界的真状。我们或者会想山差·邦札是神经健全的，可以当个标准来量他主人神经错乱的程度。简直不是这么一回事；山差·邦札在他特别方面是同他主人一样地疯的。若使那个是给幻想弄糊涂了的，这个便可以说是被常识弄糊涂的了，那可笑的行为是同样的。这种情形可以在那海岛的问题上很清楚地看出，那海岛是当吉诃德先生得到王国时候，要托山差去管理的。虽然任何胡闹的生意人的大话山差都可以看穿，他却立刻承认他主人是没有私心，诚实不欺，对他所说关于海岛的事情完全相信。他对于这海岛计划用了好多的心思，发表了许多的批评。有时他宣布总督的地位同他很不合式，说他的老婆一定做不出一个很大方的总督太太。有时他却

---

2 cut a poor figure: make a bad impression.

times he vehemently asserts that many men of much less ability than himself are governors, and eat every day off silver plate[1]. Then he hears that, if an island should not come to hand, he is to be rewarded with a slice of a continent, and at once he stipulates that his domain shall be situated on the coast, so that he may put his subjects to a profitable use by selling them into slavery. It is not a gloss upon Cervantes to say that Sancho is mad; the suggestion is made, with significant repetition, in the book itself. "As the Lord liveth", says the barber, addressing the squire, "I begin to think that thou oughtest to keep him company in the cage, and that thou art as much enchanted as he. In an evil day wast thou impregnated with his promises, and it was a sorrowful hour when the island of thy longings entered thy skull."

So these two, in the opinion of the neighbours, are both mad, yet most of the wisdom of the book is theirs, and when neither of them is talking, the book falls into mere commonplace. And this also is many times recognised and commented on in the book itself. Sometimes it is the knight, and sometimes the squire, whose conversation makes the hearers marvel that one who talks with so much wisdom, justice, and discernment should act so foolishly[2]. Certainly

---

1 eat... off silver plate：直译作"由银盘里吃去东西"。

热烈地说好多材〔才〕干不如他的人都做了总督,天天用银盘吃饭。后来他听说若使得不到海岛,会赏他大陆上一块地,他立刻先行说好他的领土要在海边,为的他可以在他的人民身上发财,把他们卖了当奴隶去。说山差是疯了,并不是替塞文狄斯辩护;这种含蓄的意思在那本书里也可以看出,而且有意地重覆说着。"真真的",理发匠对从卒说,"我开始想你应当跟他同在笼里;你同他是一样地给什么东西迷住了。在一个不幸的日子,你心中得到他那给你做海岛总督的允许,当你所心想的海岛这个观念跑到你头里时候,这是个可以悲哀的时间。"

所以这两个人由他们邻居看来都是疯的,但是这书里大部分的聪明思想都是他们的,当他们都不说话的时候,那书就降到仅仅平常的作品了。这意思在书的本身里面也常常承认过,点了出来。有的是武士,有的是从卒说的话使听的人觉得奇怪,说话说得这么聪明公平,透澈的人,做事竟会傻到那样子。真

---

2 who talks... so foolishly:参看 44 页"who seemed... natural benevolence"注中最后几句。

the book is a paradise of delightful discourse wherein all topics are handled and are presented in a new guise. The dramatic setting, which is the meaning of the book, is never forgotten; yet the things said are so good that when they are taken out of their setting they shine still, though with diminished splendour. What could be better than Don Quixote's treatment of the question of lineage, when he is considering his future claim to marry the beautiful daughter of a Christian of paynim King? "There are two kinds of lineage, " he remarks. "The difference is this—that some were what they are not, and others are what they were not; and when the thing is looked into I might prove to be one of those who had a great and famous origin, with which the King, my father-in-law who is to be, must be content." Or what could be wiser than Sancho's account of his resignation of the governorship? "Yesterday morning I felt the island as I found it, with the same streets, houses, and tiles which they had when I went there. I have borrowed nothing of nobody, nor mixed myself up with the making of profits, and though I thought to make some profitable laws, I did not make any of them, for I was afraid they would not be kept, which would be just the same as if they had never been made." Many of those who come across the pair in the course of their wanderings fall under the fascination of their talk. Not only so, but the world of imagination in which the two wanderers live proves so attractive, the infection of their ideas is so

的，那本书是有趣谈话的天堂，书里什么题目都是用一种新眼光来谈论，用新外表呈现在我们面前。戏剧式的背景，就是说这本书的真意，是永远不会忘记的；但是所说的话是那么好，就是由那背景里拿了出来，那话也是很夺目的，虽然没有放在书里时候那么灿烂。什么当他自己想着将来同一位基督教或者异教的公主求婚的名义，什么话能够比吉诃德先生谈到门第问题时所说的更妙呢？"世上有两种门第"，他说，"那不同的地方是——有种人现在虽然不阔，而从前却是阔过的，还有是从前虽然不阔，现在却阔起来了的；所以当考究这件事情的时候，我也可以成为一个由高贵著名的门第出身的人，使那国王，我将来的丈人，一定会满意。"什么话能比山差辞总督之职的报告更聪明呢？"昨天早上我离开那海岛，岛的情形同我到的时候是一样的，街道房屋盖瓦还是那么样子。我没有向谁借过钱，自己也没有跑去混钱，虽然我想定几条可以挣钱的法律，但是我怕这些法律不能实行，那就同没有定一样，所以我一条也没有定。"这对英雄在漫游中所碰的人们里好多给他们的谈话迷住了。不止这样，而且这两个漫游人所住的想像世界现出来这么可爱，他们思想的传导是这么强烈，所以还没有到末卷时候，

strong, that, long before the end of the story is reached, a motley company of people, from the Duke and Duchess down to the villagers, have set their own business aside in order to take part in the make-believe, and to be the persons of Don Quixote's dream. There was never any Kingdom of Barataria, but the hearts of all who knew him were set on seeing how Sancho would comport himself in the office of Governor, so the Duke lent a village for the prupose, and it was put in order and furnished with officers of State for the part that it had to play. In this way some of the fancies of the talkers almost struggle into existence[1], and the dream of Don Quixote makes the happiness it does not find.

Nothing in the story is more touching than the steadily growing attachment and mutual admiration of the knight and the squire. Each deeply respects the wisdom of the other, though Don Quixote, whose taste in speech is courtly, many times complains of Sancho's swarm of proverbs.[2] Each is influenced by the other; the knight insists on treating the squire with the courtesies due to an equal, and poor Sancho, in the end, declares that not all the governments of the world shall tempt him away from the service of his beloved master. What, then, are we to think, and what does their creator think, of

---

1 struggle into existence: become realized.

一大堆不同的人们，由公爵公爵夫人一直到村里人，早已把自己的事情搁在一边来弄这以假为真的把戏，变做吉诃德先生迷梦里面的人物。世上找不出一个像把拉替力亚的国，但是知道山差的人们非常想知道他当总督时候的行动，所以公爵为这个目的，借个乡村给他，把这村布置得很好，也设有国家官员预备弄这个把戏。这样子，这两位说空话者的幻想差不多能够实现一些出来，找不到的幸福，就由吉诃德先生的梦来制造。

书里面没有一件事比武士同从卒渐渐的互相亲爱，互相赞美这回事更为动人。每个人深深地尊敬对方的智慧，虽然吉诃德先生因为在说话上爱那温文有致的官话，好几次不满意山差那种一大堆的俗语。每个人都受对方的影响；武士坚持着用平等的礼遇对待他的从卒，使那可怜的山差最后声明就是把世界上所有的国家都拿给他管理，也不能引诱他使他离开，不再伺候这可爱的主人。那么对这嘴里随便说聪明话的两个傻子，我

---

2 Sancho's swarm of proverbs：山差是常识发达的人，所以熟语特别多；吉诃德先生豪爽英迈，步步模仿古宫庭中的武士，所以出语文雅。

those two madmen, whose lips drop wisdom? "Mark you, Sancho," said Don Quixote, "there are two kinds of beauty—one of the soul, and another of the body. That of the soul excelleth in knowledge, in modesty, in fine conduct, in liberality and good breeding; and all these virtues are found in, and may belong to, an ugly man... I see full well, Sancho, that I am not beautiful, but I know also that I am not deformed, and it is enough for a man of honour to be no monster; he may be well loved, if he possesses those gifts of soul which I have mentioned." Sometimes, at the height of his frenzy, the knight seems almost inspired. So, when the shepherds have entertained him, he offers, by way of thanks, to maintain against all comers the fame and beauty of the shepherdesses, and utters his wonderful little speech on gratitude:

"For the most part, he who receives is inferior to him who gives; and hence God is above all, because he is, above all, the great giver; and the gifts of man cannot be equal to those of God, for there is an infinite distance between them; and the narrowness and insufficiency of the gifts of man is eked out[1] by gratitude."

There cannot be too much of this kind of madness. Well may Don Antonio cry out on the bachelor Sampson, who dresses himself as

---

1 eked out: supplied.

们要作何感想，创造这两个人物的作者又要作何感想？"你要注意，山差，"吉诃德先生说，"天下有两种美——灵魂的美同肉体的美。智识，谦恭，良好的行为，慷慨，以及好教养，这些好处都是属于灵魂的美的；一个外貌很丑的人可以有这么多美德。……我很明白，山差，我长得不漂亮，但是我也知道我没有残疾，一个有体面的人只要不像个妖怪也就行了；若使他有我上面所说那灵魂的好处，他便会得人家的敬爱了。"有时，当他的疯狂到了极点，这位武士差不多像个得了灵感的人。所以当牧羊人招待他以后，他为着要谢他们，献身来坚决地主张牧羊女郎的令名和美丽，去反抗一切有旁的意思的来人，他还说出他那关于感谢的奇怪的短篇演说：

"大概，赠与的人是比接收的人高一等；因为上帝是个超乎一切人之上的大赠与者，所以上帝比一切人都要高一等；人们的礼物不能够同上帝的礼物相比，因为中间有无限长的矩〔距〕离；接收的人的感谢可以补偿人们礼物的有限同不及的地方。"

这种疯颠〔癫〕，我们只怕其不多。当单身汉森卜新穿上"银月武士"的衣服，在争斗中打倒吉诃德先生的时候，亚东尼乌先

the Knight of the Silver Moon and overthrows Don Quixote in fight:

> "O sir, may God forgive you the wrong you have done to all the world in desiring to make a sane man of the most gracious madman that the world contains! Do you not perceive that the profit which shall come from the healing of Don Quixote can never be equal to the pleasure which is caused by his ecstasies?"

What if the world itself is mad, not with the ecstasy of Don Quixote, nor with the thrifty madness of Sancho, but with a flat kind of madness, a makeshift compromise between faith and doubt? All men have a vein of Quixotry somewhere in their nature. They can be counted on, in most things, to follow the beaten path of interest and custom, till suddenly there comes along some question on which they refuse to appeal to interest; they take their stand on principle, and are adamant. All men know in themselves the mood of Sancho, when he says:

> "I have heard the preachers preach that we should love our Lord for himself alone, without being moved to it by the hope of glory or the fear of pain; but, for my own part, I would love him for what he is able to do for me."

These two moods, the mood of Quixote and the mood of Sancho, seem to divide between them most of the splendours and most of the

生骂他的话一些也不错：

"啊，先生，你想把世界上最可爱的疯子变成个明白人，你这种损害全世界人类的罪过，希望上帝能够赦你！你看见没有，把吉诃德先生医好后所得的利益绝对赶不上他疯狂所给我们的快乐？"

若使全世界不像吉诃德先生那样疯起来，也不像山差那样发财疯，却是有一种平凡乏味的疯狂，一个在信仰同怀疑中间将就的折中妥协办法，那岂不是更糟吗？一切人性质里都带点吉诃德的气脉。在好多事情里，我们可以算出他们是计较利害，按照习惯，跟着老路走，等到忽然间来了问题，那时他们不肯再去计较利益；他们采取一种主义，坚持到底同金刚石一样地硬。一切人都知道自己有山差这种心情，当山差说：

"我曾经听到说教〔牧〕师说我们应当爱上帝本身，不要给〔为〕光荣的希望或者苦痛的恐惧所动而去爱上帝；但是，就我个人而言，我是因为上帝能够替我干什么事情，才去爱上帝的。"

这两种心情，吉诃德的心情同山差的心情，好像将人生大部分的光荣同大部分的安逸，一边分一半去。给一种心情完全占住

comforts of human life. It is rare to find either mood in its perfection. A man who should consistently indulge in himself the mood of the unregenerate[1] Sancho would be a rogue, though, if he preserved good temper in his doings, he would be a pleasant rogue. The man who should maintain in himself the mood of Quixote would be something very like a saint. The saints of the Church Militant[2] would find no puzzle and no obscurity in the character of the Knight of La Mancha. Some of them, perhaps, would understand, better than Don Quixote understood, that the full record of his doings, compiled by Cervantes, is both a tribate to the saintly character, and a criticism of it. They certainly could not fail to discover the religious kernel of the book, as the world, in the easy confidence of its own superiority, has failed to discover it. They would know that whoso loseth his life shall save it; they would not find it difficult to understand how Don Quixote, and, in his own degree, Sancho, was willing to be a fool, that he, and the world with him, might be made wise. Above all, they would appreciate the more squalid misadventures of Don Quixote, for unlike the public, which recognises the saint by his aureole, they would know, none better, that the way they have chosen is the way of contempt, and that Christianity was nursed in a manger.

---

1 unregenerate: 执迷不悟，顽固。
2 Church Militant: Christians on earth, regarded as warriors against evil.

了的人是很不容易找出来的。一个从头到底总是怀着这老不长进的山差的心情的人会成个无赖汉，虽然若使在一切动作中他还保持一种好脾气，他到〔倒〕是一个有趣味的无赖汉。一个存吉诃德心情的人会变做很像一个圣人。世上基督教会的圣人们对这位拉曼差的武士的性格不会觉得有什么莫名其妙看不清楚的地方。有些圣人或者会比吉诃德先生知道得更明白，相信塞文狄斯所编的吉诃德先生动作的全部记录是对圣人性格的一个贡献，同一个批评。他们一定会看出这部书里宗教的真髓，好像世俗人当很容易地相信自己的高明时候，忽略过看不出一样。他们懂得谁失丢了生命就会救这生命；他们一定不觉得困难去了解为什么吉诃德先生同在他相当程度的山差自己愿意当傻子，为的是这样子，他自己同世界能够变成聪明些。最重要的是他们会鉴赏吉诃德先生那更龌龊的灾祸，因为不像那班根据光轮来认识圣人的群众，他们这些圣人只知道他们所拣的路是受人侮辱的路，基督教是在马槽里养育起来的。